"The magical world of Maple Hollow is brilliantly realized, with every nook and cranny overflowing with vibrant energy and atmosphere. A highly inventive work, packed to the brim with surprise portals, ancient traditions, and dream worlds. A compelling metaphysical adventure story." – The BookLife Prize

"A riveting read. An immersive experience into the world of enchantment, dreams, transformation, and a coming of age whereby we can choose to trust the power of our intuition and spirit guides to come home to ourselves." – Lisa Tahir, Author of *The Chiron Effect: Healing Our Core Wounds through Astrology, Empathy, and Self- Forgiveness*

"From the very first pages, I was captivated by the enchanting symbolism and vivid imagery of this marvelously metaphysical mystery. The mystical story and themes wove their magick around me, drawing me into the world of Maple Hollow. I felt an instant connection with its rich, relatable characters, each possessing a unique old soul quality. I eagerly anticipate returning to explore its magick and mysteries further." – Vivyana, The Dragon Mystic and Bestselling Author of *Manifesting Magical Moments: Embrace the Extraordinary in Everyday Life*

"A beautifully descriptive book to transport you through the mysterious story. Clever weaving of the importance of dreams, synchronicities and trusting in the unknown." – Josephine Sorciere, The Evolutionist, Author of *2020: The Alchemists' Awakening*

THE DREAM HAUNTERS

A METAPHYSICAL MYSTERY OF MAGICK

MEGAN MARY

INNER REALMS PUBLISHING

Copyright © 2024 by Megan Mary Iudice
Published by Inner Realms Publishing

For more information contact: Inner Realms Publishing
info@innerrealmspublishing.com

MeganMary.com

Book cover by Dragana Nikolic

Illustration by Melissa Rankin

Editing by Ivywild Editing & Writing Services LLC

979-8-9900882-2-1

979-8-9900882-1-4 (paperback)

979-8-9900882-0-7 (ebook)

Library of Congress Control Number: 2024909478

Across the realms, this book is dedicated to the feline companions I've had the privilege of sharing my life with: Nutmeg, Zooti, Mystera, Milu & Merlin.
Your magick will be with me always.

To my husband, who has consistently championed my artistic endeavors, joined me on countless walks while we hashed out plot details over the past decade, patiently listened to my endless musings on potential storylines, skillfully identified plot gaps, and inspired me with his musical innovation.

CONTENTS

A Note to the Reader   IX

1. The Storm   1

2. The Shift   5

3. The Invitation   10

4. The Crossroads   19

5. The Accident   29

6. The Manor   32

7. The Detective   49

8. The Hollow   55

9. The Lantern   64

10. The Passage   67

11. The Gift   70

12. The Library   77

13. The Letter   91

14. The Otherworld   97

15. The Following Fog   108

16. The Secret Room   114

17. The Book   116

18. The Cabin   122

19. The Frequencies   132

20. The Dimensions   144

21. The Key   152

22. The Island   155

23. The Café   160

24. The Poison   166

25. The Moon   168

26. The Veil   170

27. The Reunion   180

28. The Pumpkin Patch   186

29. The Hollow   198

30. The Familiars   202

31. The Legacy   205

Epilogue   208

Acknowledgments   210

About the Author   211

A Note to the Reader,

Thank you so much for your interest in the mysterious and magickal world of Maple Hollow.

In 2014, I had a vivid and unique dream that was so real it became the inspiration for this story. Yet, like so many writers, after writing the first 10,000 words, I abandoned the story, unsure if anyone would ever read it.

After battling chronic disease for many years and going through a number of amazing spiritual experiences, I began to listen to the whispers of my dreams. Then I went back to the story I had written all those years ago. To my amazement, it started to take on a whole new life and direction. I now feel driven to spread awareness of the value of dreams and their capacity for transformation. I merged this passion with my persistent fascination with the unknown, mysteries, Celtic mythology, along with my love of Halloween, and my lifelong connection to cats, to create this story. I hope it will enchant and enlighten you on your journey.

In love and light,

Megan Mary

CHAPTER ONE

THE STORM

OCT 12, 2007

I t was the dark of night. Jewelia sat facing a round altar in the library of the grand Skye Manor. Raindrops slowly chased each other down the windowpanes. Her hair was long, dark, and shiny, like the reflection of the moon. Her eyes were deep green, reflecting the glow of candlelight that surrounded her. A gentle plume of smoke steadily rose from a black incense stick. It was gathered with half a dozen others inside a small vase. Next to it lay a deck of cards illustrated with a pentacle surrounded by knotwork.

The altar was covered with crystals, stones, books, and candles of all different shapes and sizes. Fat black candles squatted near tall red ones. Tiny bottles with ornate lids stood next to large obelisk-shaped crystals. Silver runes, small glass balls, and random strings of beads intermingled with the candles and crystals. A white sage stick and an ornate oil lamp fought for room in the cluttered space. Behind her loomed the tall shadow of a floor-to-ceiling bookshelf filled with thousands of books. A wooden rolling ladder leaned against the shelves. The sound of rain filled the room, gently tapping on the four-pane window. Heavy black curtains accented the deep purple walls, the velvet gathered on either side by silky amethyst ropes.

Jewelia was concentrating, deeply focused on something, but she seemed tired and worn. Curled up on her lap was a small black cat. His fur was dark as a galaxy, and his eyes as bright as stars. She chanted and repeated words that were barely audible. In one hand she held a scrying pendulum that hung from a long black chain, and in the other she grasped a smooth hematite stone, candlelight reflecting in its shiny surface. The purple crystal pendulum slowly spun widdershins, heeding her whispered words.

She sat silently, her eyes closed. Time passed slowly as she breathed in and out, in rhythm with the breath of the cat. They were one breath, passing through time.

A sudden clap of thunder broke the silence. Jewelia's eyes snapped open. Jarred out of her placid place of meditation, she reached for a pad of paper. She wrote and then stopped, holding her pen just away from the paper as if in a channeled trance, then continued on, only to stop again a few words later. Once her words had fully inked the page, she folded the letter and placed it in a small white envelope. She firmly pressed a stamp into the red wax simmering nearby, sealed the envelope, and wrote

Hannah

in large letters in the middle.

She rose quickly from her seat, the cat springing off her lap. She ran out to the foyer, then down the long dark hallway toward the back door, grabbing a cloak hanging on a nearby hook and departing from the shelter of her home.

Skye Manor sat in the middle of an enormous, circular pumpkin patch. There was one straight path that led from the manor through the center of the patch, ending at the sea. This path was lined on both sides with immensely tall cypress trees. They stood like guards, perfectly lined up, creating a dark corridor to the water. Jewelia ran down this corridor toward the shore, cutting through the patch.

The storm swirled around her, thunder cracking and breaking across the sky. She headed for the dock, heart pounding in her chest. The wind whipped the trees, making them swirl as if they would be lifted right out of their roots, their branches thrashing to and fro. The rain beat on Jewelia's head and shoulders as she approached the dock.

On the dock, she knelt down and reached for the ropes that held the rowboat, her long black hair wet and matted against her face. She untangled them one by one until the small craft was freed from its attachments. It bobbed up and down on the rough water, ready to float away of its own accord. Steadying herself on a wooden dock post wrapped in weathered rope, Jewelia stepped into the boat, first her right foot, then her left. She sat on the wet wooden seat and fished around for the oars below her.

She began to row, pushing and straining the muscles in her arms, heaving back and bracing her legs. She was rowing as hard and fast as she could. She made it away from the dock and headed south, along the shore, further and further from the manor and around the bend of the tiny island. The rain fell harder and harder, as if it were trying to prevent her from proceeding any further. But she paddled on, exerting herself as much as she could.

As she rowed, she began to chant—softly at first, the words a whisper under her heavy breath. They formed a rhythm of their own as they dropped from her lips into the foggy air that had begun to envelope both her and the boat. She started to chant louder, the words becoming an incantation, carrying her emotions on the wind, swirling around her and rising out of her body.

Suddenly, a colossal thunderclap boomed above her, followed by a magnificent strike of lightning. White light, as bright as if she stood next to the moon itself, surrounded her, and then there was total silent darkness.

Jewelia had vanished.

Chapter Two

THE SHIFT

Oct 19, 2007

"I'm so sorry, dear, but we've decided to take a different direction for our dinner hour entertainment," Ms. Gardenia said from across the metal bistro table. "I do hope you understand it's not personal. Your playing is just lovely," she added, trying to soften the blow. But Hannah didn't hear that part—all she heard was the *I'm so sorry*, and all she felt was a sinking knowing in her gut that something else had happened she had no control over.

I'm so sorry was something everyone said to her, a lot. When her parents died, when her grandmother died after that. She was used to losing, used to being pitied, used to feeling kicked out of places whenever she got comfortable. She was used to feeling there was no real place for her. That dark, dreaded feeling of emptiness and of being lost started creeping over her like a shadow.

"Oh, no problem," she replied, her gut churning, her innate self-defenses ramping into full gear as another rejection reared its ugly head. *I don't need this job*, she immediately thought to herself. *I'll find another one,* the voice in her head assured her.

She stood up and pushed her chair in. It squeaked loudly against the floor as she rose, and the centerpiece of orange mums on the table rocked back and forth. She had worked at the Midnight Lounge in Morningside as a pianist since she finished her music degree a few years back. She loved the atmosphere at the Lounge when it was bustling with people in the evening, with its soft candlelight, velvet couches, and the sweet tinkling of wine glasses as patrons shared secrets and smiles. But now, in the harsh light of her firing, the restaurant took on a whole new feeling of rejection and exclusion.

"You can pick up your check next Friday, or I can mail it to your address, whatever you prefer," Ms. Gardenia said. A cloud of stale perfume hung above her over-sprayed, sticky hair, immovable against the gentle breeze from the ceiling fan. Her imitation satin blouse was a bit too tight for her buxom stature.

"You can mail it, thanks."

Hannah walked calmly out of the lounge, leaving her sheet music behind on the piano bench. It was too much. She had put up a good front, but her heart sank and she wanted to be alone, anywhere but there.

She rode her bike back to her apartment as quickly as she could. The sun had already set beyond the horizon as she flew through her small mountain town, but Hannah wore her sunglasses anyway to hide her streaming tears. As she slammed her bike against the siding of her apartment building, nearly toppling the pumpkins lined up in a row by the front door, she could see that her roommate Maggie's car was gone. A sigh of relief washed over her; she could at least have privacy to wallow in her disappointment.

She headed to her room as fast as she could and dropped onto the bed in a heap of heavy sorrow. Without her job at the Lounge, she'd have no way to pay her rent. Maggie had been trying to convince her to let her boyfriend move in, and Hannah had not been keen on the idea, but now she would have to agree. If she couldn't find another job, she would have to move out. She would lose her home and be miserable, again.

Exhausted from feeling that the universe was conspiring against her, and wallowing in her frustration at her inability to control her own destiny, Hannah drifted off to sleep.

A slivered crescent moon glowed in the sky. A narrow cloud crawled through the middle. In the distance, ravens and crows cawed, and the rustle of leaves crumbling in the wind filled her ears. The air was dank with fog, and the ground was moist. Hannah's feet, bare and cool, made impressions in the mud and grass as she walked.

Thick vines gathered around her ankles, intertwined and covering the ground like dense seaweed at the bottom of a dark sea. The vines were never-ending, it seemed, running deep within the soil and tangling onto each other on all sides. They were sturdy, bright green, coursing with life, and shaded with enormous ruffled leaves that jetted out from their stems to rise above the green furry pipelines. Yellow flowers yet to blossom peaked out from barely opened sprouts, and long, wheat-like fronds with pollen-filled seedlings wrapped and knotted themselves among the vines and leaves.

Magnificent pumpkins rose between the vines and leaves. They were gigantic, enormously round, brilliantly orange, and adorned with shadowy rivets and indentations from top to bottom and on all sides. Each was crowned with a fantastic stem connecting it to the pipeline of pulsating life force. There were pumpkins of nearly every color: some orange, some peach, some white, some yellow, some that were bumpy orange with green flecks. The fog, thick and wide, gently nestled itself among the pumpkins. The deep green vines were teaming with energy. They began to pulsate and move like snakes, wrapping around her ankles first, then crawling up her legs. As they quickly wrapped around her legs she felt grounded, supported, connected. A buzz encircled her body, waves of electric vibration bounding through her. It was a network! A pumpkin patch neural network. She was part of it, and it was part of her. It was alive and she felt its life force running through her. She did not hesitate or attempt to detach herself. She felt invigorated and infused with an energy greater than herself. It made her feel super-charged, powerful, and enchanted.

Hannah woke up with a start, catching her breath. Her legs still shimmered from the vibration. She'd had this dream before; in fact, this was a recurring dream that she'd had since childhood. She still couldn't figure out what it meant. It haunted her, like a shadow following her on a dark street. But it also had begun to feel comforting, like an old song.

CHAPTER THREE

THE INVITATION

I t was still before dawn, the world quiet and dark. The heater hummed a soothing wind from the register in the floor. Through the curtains, Hannah could see the moon. It was an exact half, like those half-moon cookies she'd seen at a bakery yesterday afternoon. Her stomach grumbled at the thought of warm pastry. She crawled out of bed, reached for her bathrobe, slipped into her slippers, and proceeded down the hall to the kitchen. She fixed herself a warm cup of chai, snatched the brown bag from the bakery with her pumpkin spice muffin that had been waiting patiently on the kitchen counter, and plopped down on the tattered armchair nearest the kitchen. The cushions were covered in a deep purple velvet that went well with the antique legs and arms. She had bought it at a thrift shop over the summer and it had a regal feel to it, even though it was worn and secondhand.

Hannah liked to start her day alone. There was a sense of peace she could never find during the rest of the day, once the sun broke through the window and everyone started on their bustling way. The apartment was small but quaint. In the early mornings it was like she didn't even have a roommate, since Maggie was almost always fast asleep at this hour, being more of a night owl than she was.

Opening up her laptop, Hannah typed "recurring dreams" into the search engine. She read the top results without clicking on any of the links. One of them said, "recurring dreams are an indication that you are ignoring a message being sent. Until you pay attention, it will continue to happen."

She went back to the search engine and typed in "dream meanings." The first result was a link to a dream dictionary. She clicked.

Once the page loaded, she clicked on the letter V and paged down past "vacation," "veins," and "vibrations" till her eyes stopped on "vines." There were a number of interpretations, depending on whether she was climbing them or being tied down by them. It said that if you see vines in your dream, it means you feel like you're always right and advising others when your opinion is not requested.

She hit the back button and clicked on P. The pumpkins in the dream had been very prominent. It being October, Hannah hadn't given much thought at first to this. As she took another bite of her pumpkin muffin, she paged past "parents," "peacocks," and "pets" till she arrived at "pumpkin." The dictionary said that pumpkins imply you have health issues. Or it could also be a sign of prosperity at home. Hannah wasn't ill and also wasn't prosperous, especially having just lost her job. Her stomach grumbled—perhaps at the sugar she'd mindlessly consumed, or perhaps it was frustration at not finding helpful answers.

She scrolled back up again and clicked on M, paging past "magnet" and "medicine" till she got to "moon."

Apparently seeing a crescent moon in a dream indicated a son. Hannah thought it was strange. She didn't have a son, and didn't intend to have children. So this one didn't apply to her either.

She leaned back in the armchair and had another gulp of chai. Her mind began to wander back and forth, from the dream to her day ahead.

She reached across to a nearby end table for the stack of mail she'd picked up yesterday afternoon. She rifled through the junk mail, tossing advertisements on the floor to be discarded, stopping when she came upon a handwritten manila envelope. Hannah didn't recognize the handwriting, but it was addressed to her. She tore it open to find a standard-size white one inside. It bore a red wax seal, and on the front it simply read

Hannah

She noticed that the handwriting on the inner one was significantly different from the handwriting on the outer one. On the outside her address was written in smallish, non-cursive printing; but inside her name was written in an elaborate calligraphy style.

Hannah sliced the envelope open and quickly unfolded the contents to reveal a handwritten letter. But she could not read the elaborate scrawls. She wondered if it was some sort of foreign language she didn't know, or if there was some sort of mistake. She noticed that within the red wax seal there was a small symbol. It was shaped like a key, but the old kind, a skeleton key. It was gilded and round on top, with several smaller tips toward the bottom. It was tilted, and crossing over it was a treble clef.

She flipped the letter over and examined the back, but there was nothing there either. Picking up both envelopes again, she scanned them for any other information or instruction. Only then did she notice the return address: it read *Jewelia Skye, Maple Hollow.*

"Jewelia Skye?" Hannah said out loud. That was her aunt. Technically, her long-lost aunt, her father's sister. She knew *of* Jewelia more than she knew her, though, since she'd never actually met her. She remembered that Jewelia lived somewhere in New England, which seemed like the other side of the world to Hannah, who had always lived in the mountains out West. Occasionally, as a child, she would find cards from her aunt in the mail around birthdays and holidays. Her father's relationship with his sister had always been distant—when he did refer to her, he'd use words like "eccentric" or "batty." He was rather dismissive of her, although Hannah had never quite understood why.

Her parents had died before Hannah was old enough to ask about it. Their car drove off Lone Peak Cliff and landed in the rocky depths below. But the cause of the accident was never determined. Hannah intrinsically felt there was more to the story than she was being told. She had a sense she just couldn't shake that her parents were not gone. Ever since their passing, she had felt their spirits around her, as if they were watching everything. There were so many unanswered questions she had about what really happened.

As she turned all the papers over thoughtfully, she suddenly realized there was something else. Folded inside was an airline voucher. It had her name printed on it and read, *Good for one one-way plane ticket from the bearer's city of choice to Maple Hollow. Non-refundable. Non-transferable. Does not expire.*

As Hannah sat there, perplexed, a noise roused her—it was her phone ringing. Her heart quickened as she jumped to grab it before it could wake Maggie. "Hello?" she croaked.

"Is this Hannah Skye?" came the robotic voice of a woman.

"Yes, this is Hannah," she said cautiously, wondering who in the world was calling, much less at this time of day.

"My name is Detective Norma Nyx with the Coastal Investigations Department in Maple Hollow."

"Detective?" Hannah's heart began pounding in her chest. "Maple Hollow?" she added searchingly. That was where her aunt lived. Had something happened to her aunt?

"Your aunt, Jewelia Skye, has been reported as a missing person. I'm the lead investigator on this case, so I'm contacting any known relatives to try to track down her whereabouts."

"Aunt Jewelia Skye," Hannah repeated, not meaning to say it out loud but contemplating as the words rang out. She really couldn't make sense of why her parents had been so secretive about Jewelia. Were they embarrassed by her? Or maybe they just didn't understand her well enough to want her to be part of their lives. Her father had insisted on making his own way as an adult, separating himself from his family. Hannah suddenly focused on the second bit of information. "Missing?!"

"Yes, last week we had a very big storm here in Maple Hollow," the detective responded. "No one has seen her since that night."

"Oh, that's terrible—is there anything I can do?"

"Have you been contacted by your aunt, or do you know anyone who has been?"

"Oh, not at all. I actually have never been in contact with her," Hannah replied.

"Ah, well, if you hear anything, please get in touch with me." The detective gave Hannah her phone number.

"Sure, of course," Hannah agreed, and hung up.

She was still holding the letter from her aunt in her hand, but had chosen not to reveal anything to the detective. After what had happened to her parents, she didn't trust investigations, disappearances, or detectives; she was not about to let them know anything about anyone she cared about. What would she say, anyway? That she had a letter she couldn't read, or a plane ticket? She would keep this to herself until she figured out what it meant and learned more about what had happened.

Her dream flashed through her mind. The pulsating vines wrapping around her ankles and the exhilarating life force surging through her. She wondered what she should do. Aunt Jewelia obviously wanted her to come to Maple Hollow for a reason. She must have sent the letter before she disappeared, Hannah figured. Or perhaps she didn't disappear at all? Maybe something else had happened to her. Maybe she was trying to send a warning about something. Hannah felt her suspicions rise.

She set down her aunt's letter and picked up the rest of the mail. The next piece was the bill for the rent. She flinched as she remembered the events of yesterday, Ms. Gardenia serendipitously relieving her of her job as a pianist. The feeling of dread and anxiety flooded her blood again as she thought about how she didn't have a way to pay her rent.

What was she going to do? She had no real family. Well...she did, sort of. Jewelia was her family; in fact, the only family left that she knew of. She had to find out what had happened to her aunt. She would use that plane ticket voucher before anyone found out about it—she would travel to Maple Hollow to get to the bottom of this. But where would she stay?

She did remember her father mentioning someone else who lived with her aunt...a caretaker of sorts he only referred to as "Old Man Adams."

Suddenly Hannah knew what to do. She jumped up, hurried to her room, and began rummaging through her closet. When her parents passed, her grandmother had given her a box of their things. She found the large box, dusted off the top, and sifted through old photo albums and newspaper clippings about the accident. Her eyes landed on her father's old address book, the black leather worn from years of use. She flipped to the S section to find her aunt's address. Below it was the phone number for Old Man Adams.

Hannah called the number. She waited anxiously as it rang, hoping he would answer.

"This is Adams," a raspy, old-man voice said on the other end.

"Hello! My name is Hannah Skye. I'm Jewelia's niece." Her greeting started in an awkward and cautious tone.

"Yes, of course...Hannah!" he said after a moment, and with a bit of charm.

"I just got a call from Detective Norma Nyx about Aunt Jewelia's disappearance." She felt her tone become more serious.

"Oh, yes, and did you receive the letter I forwarded to you?" Old Man Adams sounded drastically different than before, his distress now obvious. "I'm so worried about her. No one has seen her since the night of the storm. I was the one who reported her missing, and then found that letter addressed to you in the library. I thought it best to keep all this within the family, if you know what I mean."

"Yes, I see...would you..." Hannah began slowly, not sure if she should discuss the letter itself. "I was thinking of coming there, to Maple Hollow, to help," she sputtered. "I, um, I lost my job yesterday and was thinking maybe if I came there, well, there must be something I can do. She's my only family."

"Of course," Old Man Adams replied softly. "You are more than welcome to stay here if you'd like. When were you thinking of coming?"

"Sunday?"

"Okay." He paused. "Let me know what I can do?"

"A ride from the airport would be great," Hannah suggested.

"You got it, little lady," Old Man Adams said. "Just let me know when you'll be arriving and I'll be there."

She hung up the phone and sat with her chai.

What was she doing? She had never been to Maple Hollow, she had never met her aunt, she had never met Old Man Adams, and she was just going to stop everything and run off to this place she'd never been and leave her current life? Yes, she was.

Hannah's thoughts swirled around what the letter might say, how mysterious her aunt had always been to her, and now this. Jewelia had disappeared in a storm? Written her a cryptic letter with a plane ticket? Hannah had never been to Maple Hollow, but she felt a strong pull to go there that she couldn't quite put into words. Something was calling her, and she was starting to listen.

CHAPTER FOUR

THE CROSSROADS

OCT 21, 2007

The chilly air descended on the long road to the airport, which was lined on each side with enormously tall and towering trees, each glowing gold and yellow in the mid-day sun.

As she stepped off the bus, Hannah tightened the scarf that was nestled around her neck, its buttery warmth blocking the snappy chill in the air. The leaves crunched beneath her black velvet boots, each resolute step she took unleashing a dusty cloud about her feet. The only other sound was her small suitcase beside her, its wheels unevenly attempting to traverse the path as she walked. Her favorite black leggings snuggly wrapped her legs, although small bursts of chilled air seeped through the fashionable but impractical (as her grandmother would have said) tears in the fabric. Her black cable knit sweater, with its overly long sleeves, served as partial coverings for her exposed hands.

Her heart thumped in her chest as her mind swirled with long-forgotten memories of her childhood. She struggled to stay focused on where she was walking, partially stepping from the sidewalk into the street

when the sidewalk ended abruptly, crumbling underneath her boot. The automatic doors to the airport slid open, anticipating her arrival as she approached the ticketing entrance.

"Are you in line?" a woman's voice asked cautiously. Hannah spun around to see the woman
standing behind her, dressed in a matronly business
suit with dark rimmed glasses. She almost looked
like security because the colors of her suit were
so drab and dull. At that moment, Hannah realized she'd been absentmindedly standing near the
check-in area but had not entered the roped-off
rows meant to usher people along. Instead, she
was standing trance-like, blocking the entrance to
it. Her daydreaming had totally distracted her and
she'd almost forgotten where she was.

"Oh...no," she sputtered, politely stepping to the
right so the woman could move past. As she went by,
Hannah gazed down at the woman's carry-on suitcase. Hanging from a string on the suitcase handle
was a small plastic tag with an interesting symbol on
it that caught her eye. It was a circle with a triangle
and a snake inside.

"Everyone please move to the front," a female voice
boomed from behind the counter. Hannah entered the
roped aisle and meandered her way through the little
maze it made toward the counter. It made her think
of the corn mazes they always created this time of
year and how much she loved finding her way through
them. She didn't much care for the scary versions
where people jumped out and tried to scare her, but
she did like the challenge of having to find her way to
the end without any clue of which way it went. It was
solving the mini-mystery that always gave her a sense

of satisfaction when she emerged at the end, finally able to see the way out.

As she made her way through security and up the long escalator to the terminal, she retraced in her mind everything she had packed. Did she remember everything on her list? Would there be a way to replace anything she'd forgotten? She decided she needed to settle down and calm her mind. She surveyed the scene and chose an open chair along the wall, far away from everyone else.

"Attention, all passengers," the overhead woman's voice boomed again, this time sounding like she was holding the microphone way too close to her mouth. "Today's flight will be delayed by forty-five minutes. We apologize for the inconvenience and want to ask that anyone with a connecting flight please check the monitors for updates. Thank you for flying with us today."

That was just what she needed. A longer travel day. Why did this always seem to happen? Hannah listened to music while she waited. She pushed the headphones into each ear and started one of her playlists. Her mind's eye swirled with a collage of colors, the music painting the fabric of her mind. She needed a good distraction to help her pass the time and filter out the annoying children and stressed-out travelers that surrounded her.

She noticed that all of the podiums had small Halloween decorations with cornstalks, pumpkins, and black cats. It softened the bland and institutional feel the airport normally had. Excitement fluttered in her chest when she thought about Halloween coming up. This was her absolute favorite time of year. In fact, she wished Halloween lasted the entire year. She always found all the myths and legends surrounding the ancient celebration so fascinating. Nowadays people thought it was just a stupid holiday for kids, or that it was all about candy. Being of Celtic heritage, Hannah's lineage was from the old world of both Ireland and Scotland. Which explained her wavy reddish hair and green eyes. "A young lassie," her grandmother would call her.

Her father was not interested in Halloween at all and would always be so dismissive when the holiday rolled around. Although he often referred to Aunt Jewelia as "off-kilter," one of the few things he did share about Maple Hollow was that it was known for having one of the largest, if not *the* largest, Halloween celebrations in the nation, called Halloween Hollow. This was a three-day event brimming with spooky themes. There was everything you could think of, from costume contests to pumpkin-carving contests, apple-bobbing events, harvest decorating, bake sales, a farmer's market, ghost walks, spine-chilling storytelling sessions, corn mazes, hayrides, mystery dinners, and more. There were also more metaphysical options such as chakra readings, tarot divinations, and crystal healing. Hannah had read about the festivities online and was excited to finally get to experience it for herself while reconnecting with her family heritage. It was the perfect time to do all this. Well, if only Aunt Jewelia were there to greet her.

Eventually the speaker boomed again: "Attention all passengers, we are now boarding at gate thirteen." Hannah barely heard the announcement over her headphones, but she saw people getting up and starting to get in line. She gathered her things and walked toward the door to the jetway. Once she boarded and got to her row, she plopped down, shoved her backpack under the seat, and went through her ritual of adjusting the air vents and lights above it. She pulled up the heavy side tray from the compartment between the seats and it smacked down on her lap, its weight surrendering from lack of proper hydraulics.

"Can I get you anything to drink?" the flight attendant asked. She was dressed in a bright red suit, perfectly laundered and pressed. Her hair was in a neat, shiny bun on top of her head, and she wore tight nude stockings and polished Mary Jane wedges on her feet.

"Apple juice?" Hannah asked, and the attendant winked.

Her thoughts of harvest time had made her crave the sweet tang of apple cider. She reached into the pocket on the seat in front of her and picked out a magazine with an autumn scene on the cover.

The plane launched itself high above her hometown, its belly lifting higher and higher into the blue sky filled with large fluffy clouds. She watched as the buildings and trees got smaller and smaller. The rivers began to look like small strokes of oil on a painting and the houses like tiny chips on a computer motherboard, some neatly lined up in rows or defined neighborhoods and others scattered about with no identifiable plan or reason. When the plane was fully enveloped in cloud and fog, and when she could no longer see out the window, she slid the hard plastic white window shade down and settled in to wait. It was going to be a long flight. She would have to change planes in Denver, and then prepare for the haul across the country to New England.

On the next leg of her journey, she sought out a magazine again. This time, she stopped on a page that caught her eye. Surprisingly enough, it was a picture from the Halloween Hollow festival in Maple Hollow. A group of people were standing in front of an enormous display of carved pumpkins, everyone smiling and looking festive. As she read the caption, Hannah's eyes stopped on the words *Jewelia Skye*.

It was in fact Aunt Jewelia. She was dressed in a flowing black velvet dress with a purple velvet scarf. Her long black hair was being lifted by a light wind. Her eyes were deep and dark and her skin was porcelain and clear, her lips red and shiny. Her boots were knee-high, black, and pointy.

Hannah shoved the magazine into her backpack. This was the only photo she actually had of her aunt, and she wanted to keep it. Having never met her, it was like she'd lost something she didn't even know she had. Her mind wandered again to all the other things she'd lost in her life.

After her parents died, she'd gone to live with her grandmother on her mother's side. Her grandmother, seeing how disconnected she was, had taken her to the local humane society to find her a friend. Hannah had felt an affinity for the cats there. They were all alone, each one having lost their family. Their eyes had a fear and a longing desperation. They'd been thrust into the world, lost and anxious, each one desperately wanting a home, a connection. She was seeking the same thing. She wanted to take them all home. She understood them. And they understood her.

She'd picked a colorful calico. The cat was so small, she could walk into Hannah's hand and fit in her pocket. Her meows were tiny and high. Hannah's heart leapt. She pressed her nose into her fur and stroked her back, one hand after the other, a smile spreading across her face. As an only child, she had always wanted a companion.

She named the kitten Mystera. They were inseparable. Mystera followed Hannah everywhere. No matter where she went, Mystera followed behind. If she was sad, Mystera would pace around her feet until she broke out of her fog and played with her. If she was tired and just wanted to rest, Mystera would curl up on her lap, whether she was sleeping or sitting. She even used to crawl up her leg when she was standing and climb all the way up to her shoulder, perching there as if she had climbed Mount Everest, surveying the world below. Hannah and Mystera were forever friends. Mystera had lived to be eleven. Hannah was devastated when she lost Mystera. Her world had another hole in it, and she felt the loss every day.

She settled deeper into her seat, pulling the thin airplane blanket around her to shield herself from the circulating air. She slowly drifted off to sleep and began to dream.

She was back in her apartment in her bedroom. Even though her bedroom was normally very organized, as she looked around there were clothes everywhere. A large pile was at the foot of her bed, another pile on top of her long white dresser, and then more piles all around her on the floor.

She was scrambling around for her clothes. She had piles everywhere of pants and tops but they were all black. In the piles she couldn't tell one from the other. She was desperately looking for something else to put on. She was headed out and would be late if she couldn't decide what to wear.

I need to change, she kept thinking as she pulled items one by one out of the piles, then threw them back in.

As she scurried about, her phone rang. She lunged to grab it off the dresser. "Hello."

"Hi, Hannah," her mother's voice smoothly greeted her.

"Mom!" Hannah chirped, a feeling of happiness rising in her heart.

"Hannah, I wanted to tell you—" her mom began.

A storm of static overtook the line. Her mom's words sounded like a distant mumble, like a radio whose dial was tuned slightly off the channel, in between stations.

Then Hannah heard a click. "Mom? Mom, are you there?" she said.

But it was silent. She must have been disconnected.

Then she suddenly found herself in a dark forest. It was late evening, when the owls began to hoot in the trees, the crickets commenced their rhythmic song, and the stars turned on their twinkle. She began to feel again like she needed to get somewhere. Except this time, it wasn't about her clothes but about her path. There were all these different paths in the woods, and she wasn't sure which one to take. She felt lost. She didn't know what direction to go and stood paralyzed by the decision. Should she turn to the right? Or take that path that led down the hill into what looked to be a more wooded area that she couldn't see well into? Or the paths that were right in front of her—they appeared worn and possibly safe, but uninteresting. Or the path on the left which led up a hill and curved around. Or should she turn around and go back?

As Hannah stood at the crossroads, a sadness overcame her. She felt so lost, without a proper direction. But she also felt anxious, like she had to choose. She knew she could not stand there forever, otherwise she would never get to wherever it was she was going. Wherever this was, she had to get there soon. It felt urgent and was making her even more anxious and perplexed.

The darkness of the wood overhead began to spread across her path in a giant shadow. She heard a snap of a branch behind her. She spun around, peering into the darkness.

A small cat came prancing up to her. It didn't stop or acknowledge her, but started on the path to the left. It was perky, its tail straight up. Its movements were so cute, so assured, so confident. It made the decision seem so simple, Hannah thought.

Without mulling it over, she moved toward the cat, following behind it, her gaze fixed on the small paw prints it left in the soil. The cat started to move faster and faster. Hannah, in turn, had to move quicker to keep up with it. She didn't want to lose it, as she was determined to find out where it was leading her.

CHAPTER FIVE

THE ACCIDENT

OCTOBER 17, 1987

It was early, and still mostly dark. Hannah's grandmother roused her from her sleep. She was confused. Her grandmother told her to get up and get dressed, that she was coming to Grandma's house and that she had to be a big girl today. She wasn't sure why. She got up, put her clothes on, grabbed her backpack that she always took to her house, and headed down to the kitchen.

Her grandmother was waiting at the kitchen table. In the other chairs were men that Hannah didn't recognize, dressed in dark uniforms. She stopped when she entered the kitchen, confused by their presence. Her mother was usually getting breakfast together by this time, and her dad was usually sitting reading the morning paper.

"Come sit down, Hannah," her grandmother said.

Hannah looked from one man to the other, then slowly pulled out a chair. The table was a heavy wood, the chairs as well. Sometimes they were just too much for her to pull out, especially since she was small for her nearly seven years. She sat down and looked across the table at the dark and serious men, a pumpkin centerpiece sitting between them.

"Hannah dear, I'm afraid we have some terrible news," her grandmother said.

"What do you mean?" Hannah asked. It was too early, and she felt half awake.

"Hannah...it's your mom and dad. They've...they've been in a car accident." Her grandmother stopped there. Hannah suddenly saw she was fighting back pain and tears, her heart breaking as she tried to find the words.

"What? Are they...are they okay?" Hannah asked, feeling her voice shake. Her chest tightened and her pulse quickened. Her legs stiffened against the wooden chair and her head started to feel light.

"Nooo," her grandmother stuttered, again not finding the words. She stood up and walked around the table to Hannah. She put her arm on Hannah's shoulder.

Hannah still didn't know what was coming next.

"I'm afraid they didn't make it." Tears started to roll down her face. "Hannah, I'm so sorry."

"What do you mean, didn't make it? Didn't make it to where?"

That night had been her parents' anniversary. Her grandmother had come over for dinner and cake, and then her parents had gone out for a "nightcap." Her grandmother had stayed to babysit. Hannah had drifted off into a deep sleep after dinner. She hadn't been entirely surprised to be woken by her grandmother that morning, since sometimes she would stay over. But she was shocked that her parents weren't home at all.

"I'm so sorry," her grandma said as she hugged her tightly. One of the detectives raised his eyebrow in surprise, almost as if to say *she's not getting it*.

Her grandmother became more direct. "My dear, they are gone. They're not coming back."

"Their car was found at the bottom of Lone Peak Cliff. No one could survive that drop," said one of the ominous men.

Hannah sat still as a stone. She suddenly felt nothing. It was as if the world had frozen in place. There was no air moving in the room, no subtle house noises around her. She was floating in a bubble. Her breath held in a vacuum in her chest. Her eyes glazed over as if she were sleepwalking.

Her grandmother was hugging her tight, but she could not feel the warmth from her. She felt paralyzed and could not move. She had entirely shut down.

Chapter Six

THE MANOR

Oct 21, 2007

"Attention all passengers," the loudspeaker boomed, jarring her from her sleep. "We will be landing soon. Please put your tray tables in their upright and locked position and prepare for arrival."

Hannah slid open the small window shade. The clouds were parting as the plane descended. The closer it drew to the ground, the more she could see lights emanating up toward the sky. But it was mostly dark, and rain obscured her view.

Moments later, the plane landed, the wheels ever so gently making contact with the pavement, deceiving the passengers, as always, as to how fast they were really going. They rounded the path toward the terminal and eventually stopped with an abrupt jolt at the gate. Hannah sent a quick text to Maggie, letting her know she had finally arrived.

She stood in the aisle, her hand clutching her bag over her shoulder, her pulse beginning to quicken in anticipation. When she reached the exit, she stepped out onto the jetway, the moist air meeting her nose like an old friend and filling her with calm.

Hannah hurried down the jetway and into the airport. She wasn't sure what Old Man Adams looked like. As she walked past the gates toward the arrivals area, her anticipation grew. She wasn't nervous, since she loved being spontaneous. Just eager.

She spotted an older gentleman standing near the baggage claim holding a sign that said *Hannah.* He was tall in stature, his white hair sneaking out beneath a tweed flat cap, round wireframe glasses obscuring his weathered skin.

As she got closer, she could see that the expression on his face was one of concern. "Mr. Adams?" she asked as she approached him.

"Hannah?" he asked.

"Yes!" Hannah exclaimed. "Nice to meet you." They shook hands obligatorily.

"How was the flight?" he asked.

"Oh, fine, considering the weather," she replied.

"We best be getting along then. I hear it's only going to get worse later." He reached to relieve Hannah of her suitcase. "We're just going 'round the corner out here, little lady." He led the way through the doors of the airport to the taxi stand.

Despite it being cold and dark outside, rain coming down, it felt clean and fresh. The air was dewy and new. They walked quickly among the raindrops to catch the next taxi in line.

"Looks like this storm is gonna be a real doozy," Old Man Adams grumbled as he opened the back door of the taxi for Hannah to enter. Once inside, she stared out the window. Raindrops sprawled like the roots of a fast-growing weed, then descended like the long legs of deep red wine cascading down an oversized cabernet glass. It reminded her of the Midnight Lounge.

She became absorbed in her inner thoughts. *Storms in nature aren't always just...in nature,* she thought. *After all, we are all part of nature, and as such, storms are part of us, and we them. When winds rise, temperatures swell, and the air fills with change, a storm is afoot. The more dramatic the storm, the more change it brings.*

She could almost taste the change in the breeze, feel it in her lungs as she breathed it in and as it wailed over her. She thought about the circumstances surrounding her aunt's disappearance. Storms wield a force no one can contain and no one can explain.

"It's going to be a rocky ride," Adams grumbled. "We'll just catch the last ferry at eight."

"Ferry?" Hannah was not sure she heard him right.

"Yeah, the ferry," he said, sounding surprised she didn't already know about it. "It's the only way to get out to the island."

"Island?" She had no idea Maple Hollow was an island. Why had her father spoken so little of his sister and the home where they grew up? "I...didn't know Aunt Jewelia lived on an island," she finally said.

Before long the taxi pulled up at the bay and they scurried across the lot to the covered waiting area. The rain was coming down harder now. There were only a few other people waiting for ferries. "Next ferry departing now! Please board," an announcement said.

"That's us!" Adams guided her down the walkway to the boat. It was a rather large ferry with more than enough room to sit down, and large windows to look out of, when it wasn't dark and raining. "Glad it's not crowded, the ferries will be buzzing when Halloween Hollow gets underway," Adams added conversationally.

"Oh yes, I read about that. I love Halloween. It's my favorite time of year." Hannah gazed out the window, her eyes glowing from the lights along the coast that glimmered in the dark.

"Then you should feel right at home," he replied.

He began to tell her bits of lore about Maple Hollow. Hannah's ears perked up when he mentioned pumpkins. "Maple Hollow is known for its pumpkin patches. It's the stuff of legends. People come from near and far every autumn to pick out their prized pumpkins."

An enchanting fog danced on the surface of the water. It swirled around like a woman wearing a large cloak, obscuring everything in its path in a gentle, enveloping cushion of white.

"Ah, see that fog there? The island is always shrouded in it," Adams said as he watched Hannah's eyes track the thickening vapors. "Some say it has a mind of its own. It reveals things. There are legends, anyway. You'll see the island is a very unique place, unlike any other. Your aunt has lived here for many years, and your family is known far and wide this time of year for their pumpkin patch."

"Pumpkin patch?" Hannah thought of her dream of the pumpkin vines. "Oh, I can't wait to see that!"

Eventually the ferry pulled into the dock and an announcement boomed, "Maple Hollow."

When Hannah took her first steps onto the island itself, she felt a tingly sensation run from her feet into her legs and up her body. She wondered if it was just anticipation, but it felt different. The vibe surrounded her and captured her whole attention. It was a buzzing feeling, like a high-level vibration. Her right ear started to ring, then her left. And she sensed something she couldn't explain.

Old Man Adams led Hannah to his car and got in the driver's seat. They pulled away from the dock and its bright street lights into the darkness of the island. The car's headlights illuminated large trees lining the road. Hannah noticed a surreal feeling as she observed the landscape, the trees wrapped around themselves as if they had grown while twisting.

The radio in the car hummed a soft jazz tune that she recognized, but then it was interrupted by fuzzy interference. Old Man Adams turned the dial in an attempt to switch to the next station, but each time he tried, there was a strange static that buzzed over the airwaves. Eventually he turned it down until it was barely audible.

As they approached the grounds of Aunt Jewelia's home, Hannah saw a tall iron gate through the rain-filled window. It was enormous, with brick columns on each side. On top of the columns were large, dark gray gargoyles. But they were not the typical scary gargoyles; rather, their ears were long and their tails were like a fox's, their eyes looking upward to the sky, their mouths curved in a pensive grin. Stone carved into wild hair peaked out around their faces like happy flames. In the middle of the gate was a symbol forged into the iron. As his headlights illuminated it, Hannah realized it was the symbol from the wax seal of her aunt's letter.

The car slowed as the iron gate slowly opened, creaking as it scraped across the paved driveway. After crossing the threshold, they drove for a short distance and when they came to a dead end, turned left. After driving an even shorter distance, they turned and came to another dead end and took a right. Then a quick left, around a bend, and then another dead end. Another quick left, around another bend, and they arrived at a clearing. On the right was a long, wide road lined on both sides with pumpkins. It looked surreal, illuminated in the glowing light from the headlights. The fog rising from the dewy grass danced among the raindrops. It seemed as if they had driven through a maze to get there.

The car slowly made its way down the long road. The grounds of Skye Manor were enormous, the property itself stretching for what seemed like miles. They at last reached what was, as expected, a grand manor. It was hauntingly beautiful, like a castle. The car pulled into the large circular driveway and came to a stop near the front doors.

Hannah wiped the fog away from her window, then rolled it down to get a closer look. The manor felt ancient, strong, and foundational with what was clearly hand-placed stones. There were turrets that graced the corners, and tall windows each with a few tiny windows above, and above that, triangular tops that came to a point. There were so many windows that Hannah could hardly count them; each had a peak above it, and the roof rose to an even higher peak. The hazy moonlight and lingering fog gave the manor an eerie look. Hannah lifted her eyes to see the moon. A dark sliver was missing from the left side. It perfectly framed the view from her window.

"Welcome to Skye Manor. This is where you'll be staying," Old Man Adams said in a limerick sort of way. "My quarters are down the road." He opened his car door.

Hannah opened hers, placing her foot on the wet driveway and stepping out of the car's warm interior.

"Hopefully you'll find it's all in order, or the best it can be," Adams continued as he lifted her tattered luggage from the trunk and led the way down the vine-covered arched entryway toward the front door, which was knotted in craftily carved wood. She followed quickly, hoping to avoid the rain but taking in the sights as she went. He unlocked the heavy door and held it open for Hannah.

Inside, Adams switched on the light. Hannah saw a grand staircase rise up from their feet, its wide steps gradually retreating into the darkness above. A black cat came running down the stairs toward them.

"This is Midnight, Aunt Jewelia's cat. He'll be happy to have some company. I've been coming over to feed him since Jewelia's been gone."

"Hello there, Midnight." Hannah bent down to pet his head.

"First things first. Follow me to the kitchen. I imagine you've worked up an appetite with the traveling. Hope you like pumpkin soup."

"That sounds wonderful," Hannah said as she followed Adams past the stairway down a long dark hallway to the back of the manor. He began clanking dishes as soon as they entered the cavernous yet cozy kitchen, setting the table for two.

Hannah was relieved she didn't have to worry about making dinner. She sank into a chair at the large wooden table. Old Man Adams served up the soup, sliced up a large loaf of rustic bread, and joined her.

"So, tell me about you, Hannah. Did you say you'd lost your job recently?" He offered her some bread.

"Oh, yes, there isn't much to tell," she began, searching for words. "I was working as a pianist at a local lounge where I live. I enjoyed the work, but I guess they were going in a different direction. My living situation is in flux, you could say."

"I see," Old Man Adams said.

"How long have you lived here?" Hannah continued swiftly, deflecting any further questions about her misfortunes.

"I've been the caretaker here since Jewelia was young. I came to live here after her parents died. I make sure the grounds are taken care of, tend to the manor...it's too much for just one person to keep up."

Hannah smiled. She had a good feeling about Old Man Adams and was already glad she'd spontaneously decided to accept Aunt Jewelia's clear invitation to Maple Hollow.

They exchanged more small talk until the soup was gone. "That was delicious, thank you," Hannah said as she brought her dish to the sink.

"There's plenty of food in the pantry for next time you're hungry." Adams pointed to a large door with gilded knobs on it.

They walked back into the foyer. A cozy golden glow illuminated the entry. "You're welcome to pick any room upstairs you'd like to stay in, except for the room at the very end of the hall," Adams said, pointing up the grand staircase. "That's Jewelia's. Let me know if you be needing anything." He winked and handed her a small piece of folded paper. "Here's my number at the groundskeeper's cottage, a map of the grounds, and the keys to the manor." He pressed a very heavy set of iron keys into Hannah's hands. "I left you a bicycle outside the back door, too, in case you need it. Since it's late, I'll leave you now. Sleep well, I'll check in with you in the morning." He retreated into the darkness beyond the front door.

Hannah stood alone, keys in hand, belly full, listening to the sound of his car roll away down the long drive. She spun around and faced the grand stairway. On her left was a cozy parlor, filled with opulent violet furniture, charming Victorian furnishings, and a beautiful grand piano. She smiled to herself and thought, *I guess I'm not the only musician in the family. Perhaps I have inherited some of my musical talent after all.* On her right was a majestic great hall.

As Hannah crossed the foyer and entered the great hall, the walls soared above her, covered in ornate wood paneling ten feet high. Above that, the walls were orange, with clusters of swords. There was a sense of long-lost legacy battles and mythical fables whispering their stories...secrets of tales forgotten in the past, struggles, defeats, and victories. *How long has my family been here?* she wondered.

In the center was a large dining table that spanned the length of the room. Beyond it, there was a beautiful fireplace made of cream stone, so large and wide that it soared above her head, with a glowing fire inside. Columns on either side were offset by a very dark black iron center which was embossed with a series of symbols. In between the columns and the hearth were carved iron pedestals; on top of each one were carved feline statues, their silver steel shimmering in the fiery glow.

There were also four female statues, two on either side of the mantelpiece. They reminded Hannah of the Venus sculpture she had seen at a museum as a child. At the time, she had stared up from her small height toward the greatness and largeness of the stone goddess that stood before her, taken aback by the strength yet gentleness, the grandness and the mystery.

As she perused the room further, she noticed that each statue stood atop a small circular platform, on which was pictured a scene of crouching figures who appeared to be kneeling or in some sort of struggle. She listened as the faint whisper of her family's past echoed from the stone.

Life-sized, hammered metal knight armor also stood on display, two on each side of the fireplace beyond the columns. Hannah stared into the depths of the inky blackness inside their shielded helmets. It was as if eyes were peering back at her out of the darkness.

At the other end of the great hall was the most dramatic feature, a large ornate pipe organ that looked as old as the manor itself. Ornate woodwork, carved into crowns and gothic flowers and skulls, ran up and around the sides. A matching bench fit perfectly into the front nook. The feet of the instrument were shaped like statuesque dragon claws and the top was like a grand chimney, metal pipes layered upon each other, almost reaching the ceiling. Three levels of keys rounded the front. She admired the craftsmanship, running her fingers across the carvings.

Her eyes were drawn toward the wall behind the organ, which was filled with wrought-iron and metal keys of all shapes and sizes, hung without any particular pattern or placement. Some were as large as her arm, others as small as an earring. Each had its own unique shape. As she drew closer, she saw that some of the keys bore number codes and unique symbols she had never seen before.

Everything seemed so medieval, ancient, and regal. Hannah had never seen a place such as this, much less imagined such a home would be owned by a relative. A sudden feeling of longing came over her. If only she'd met Aunt Jewelia before. Why had her family kept Jewelia such a secret? Why had her aunt not reached out to her until now? She had so many things she wanted to ask, so many things she needed to know about her family.

Could she stay here at the manor? Live here? She needed to know who she was, and she needed to find out what happened to Jewelia.

She stepped out of the great hall, back into the foyer. The rain pattered on the roof. Hannah had a feeling she was not alone, even though she knew Old Man Adams had left. She turned, first looking over her shoulder into the room she'd just left, then looking at the front door, then up the stairs.

She saw it. Something or someone was at the top of the stairs.

Hannah froze.

As she gazed up the stairwell, the moonlight cast a glow through the narrow windows. She suddenly realized that there were mirrors everywhere. All different shapes and sizes. They filled the walls from the first floor to the ceiling above the foyer. Gold gilded ornate mirrors, square black boring ones, large round silver ones, oval ones, and gigantic rectangular ones. The mirrors surrounded a very large painting at the top of the stairs.

She ascended the staircase slowly, each step creaking beneath her feet as she climbed. The painting was a life-sized and very realistic portrait; it still felt like someone was standing there looking straight at her. As she drew closer, Hannah confirmed it was in fact just a very well-done painting. It was a portrait of her aunt. Jewelia's hair loosely grazing her shoulders; her eyes had such depth they almost pulled you into another world. She wore a beautiful velvet dress that complimented her shape, and she was holding a set of keys—the same keys Old Man Adams had handed her, Hannah realized.

Midnight was sitting at her feet, his paws gently placed over one another, his tail wrapping around her leg like a spiral snake. His eyes glowed a deep golden green. As Hannah stood there, keys in hand, eye to eye with the portrait, she found herself talking to her aunt. "What happened to you, Aunt Jewelia? What are you trying to tell me?"

She was so tired from the trip, and badly in need of a shower and bed. She looked down the long hallway that ran in two directions at the top of the stairs. Each side was filled with closed doors, all in a row. As she followed the doors with her eyes, she noticed one was cracked open, so she began her way down the hall in that direction. Halfway down, she stopped by a mullioned picture window that overlooked the grounds.

The chill of the fall night consumed Maple Hollow, and the murky layer of fog now filled the meadow. As she gazed out, she could see Old Man Adam's cottage way off in the distance; a single plume of smoke rose from the chimney and light glowed from the inside.

A lightning bolt cracked across the sky, the brief flash of light illuminating the grounds. Hannah jumped. It was the pumpkin patch she had dreamed about. The giant pumpkins glistened in the glow of the lightning. A sprawling jungle of weaving vines and plump gourds covered everything between the cottage and the manor. All open space burst at the seams with shadowy pumpkins.

Maple Hollow is known for its pumpkin patches, Old Man Adams had told her on the ferry.

She heard a low rumble of thunder off in the distance. There was something about that sound that both quickened her pulse and gave her a bit of a chill. Perhaps it was the anticipation of the impending crash of thunder, or maybe it was just the ominous portent of it. Her stomach fluttered. What had she gotten herself into?

As she continued down the narrow hallway, she noted that even here, the walls were filled with mirrors. A starburst mirror hung low to the ground, much too low for anyone to see in it. Its circular shape was rimmed with gold and around the outside were bursts of rays jetting out like chopsticks from the center. Another mirror was white and shaped like a snowflake, its arrows pointing in all directions like a weather compass. There were ovals, squares, rectangles, some vintage, some modern. Some had heavy wooden frames and others thin metal frames, while some had no frames at all. Some had handles, like the kind that lives on dressing tables and you wouldn't usually hang on a wall. Tiny mirrors, no larger than her palm, were intermixed with the normal-to-larger-sized mirrors. Even though they looked rather chaotic on the wall, there was also some sort of order to them she couldn't quite decipher.

Why would someone surround themselves with so many mirrors? Did Aunt Jewelia love to look at herself? Was she obsessed with the way she looked? For what other reason would someone have so many mirrors? Did she always want to make sure she could see behind her? If so, who did she expect to be creeping in her shadow?

Hannah reached the door she had spotted from the top of the stairs and gently pushed it fully open. The room was quiet. It had a stately antique dresser in the corner, and a four-poster bed with tall carved spires. She dropped her bags by the door and flopped onto the bed. The sheets were creamy satin and luxuriously soft.

The thunderstorm had mellowed into a steady stream of rain. Hannah cracked open the large Victorian window by the bed and lay listening for the silence between the raindrops. As she slowly began to drift off to sleep, she turned over to adjust her pillow and felt a tingle up her spine.

She slightly opened her eyes, and something caught her gaze. There was a mirror hanging on the wall, an ornate, gold-maple-leaf-trimmed rectangular mirror above the dresser. The clouds had parted just enough for the moonlight to shine through the sheer curtains, piercing the darkness and creating a white path on the floor. As Hannah sat up to look closer, she knew there was something else in the mirror. Something that was not physically in the room. It was a figure standing in the corner. Transparent as it was, she could almost make out a face. Her heart began to pound in her chest. Her palms were dewy with perspiration. She grasped for the sheets below her, attempting to ground herself.

It didn't move, but stood solemn. She looked to the corner—there was nothing there. She looked back to the mirror and the figure was gone. She sat up even straighter now. Maybe she was just tired, maybe she was dreaming. It couldn't have been what she thought. She rubbed her eyes, stretched a bit, and convinced herself to shrug it off as imagination. Rolling over, she soon fell into a deep dream.

The silence was pierced by a loud clamoring noise. A disordered song, notes misplaced and chaotic. She got out of bed to find out where it was coming from.

Once she was in the hallway, she could hear it even louder. The light was a strange deep purple; not morning, but not still night. The sound echoed in the stairwell against the tall arched beams. Hannah headed down the stairs, each step creaking in a different way as her weight shifted. At the bottom, she turned and entered the parlor. She looked at the grand piano, and there on top of the piano's keys stood a small kitten.

His eyes turned to her immediately. His gaze fixed on her. "Hi," he chirped.

The cat's fur and tail were light gray with dark gray stripes. His ears appeared bigger than his head and his eyes were large in his face, outlined in white against his gray striped cheeks. Above and between his eyes, his stripes formed a letter M. His whiskers were white and the fine hair in his ears was white as snow. His nose was a dark gray, his eyes a deep turquoise blue.

Hannah rubbed her eyes, still standing in the foyer, and looked at him again.

"I'm Wixby. Nice to meet you!" he said with a lisp, in an adorable high voice, as he walked across the keys. Then he leaped off the keys, pushing his back legs against them to make a final clamoring, and landed on the bench.

"I'm Hannah," she replied. She entered the room and walked toward him to get a better look. When she got close enough, she stuck out her hand for him to sniff. She knew that's the best way to gain their trust, rather than rudely reaching out to touch them without a proper scent introduction.

Wixby obliged and bumped her hand with his head, slightly raising his tiny paws off the ground in confirmation.

"I know," he said confidently, still sounding small and happy. "I've been waiting for you. I live here," he continued. "Well, me and my friends."

"Your friends?" Hannah said cautiously.

"The other cats," he said in a how-do-you-not-know sort of way.

"Other cats?" she repeated, confused.

"We all live here at the manor with Jewelia."

"You know my Aunt Jewelia?"

"Of course!" he quipped. "Well, she's gone now..." His tone trailed sadly downward.

She petted his extremely soft fur. His wide eyes glowed up at her. "Do you play the piano?" he asked inquisitively.

"I do!" she exclaimed.

"Will you play for me?" he asked in a syrupy, singsongy way.

Hannah pulled out the bench and sat down. Her fingers gently grazed the keys. They were heavy ivory. She began the first notes of Beethoven's *Moonlight Sonata.*

Wixby cautiously placed his right paw on her lap, then his left, then proceeded to move his whole small body onto her lap and curl up in a ball. She could feel him purring on her thighs, his furry body filling her with warmth and she his, exchanging energy.

As she played, a force flowed out of her fingers into the piano and her heart swooned on a heavy, mournful wave. She felt filled with a sadness that ran deep into dark places.

Once she played the final notes, she slowly removed her hands from the keys.

Wixby had put his head down and was fast asleep in her lap.

She gently patted his tiny head. "Wake up, Wixby," she whispered.

His eyes slowly opened until they were wide and round, and he looked up at her.

"And now we begin," he said. He jumped up with a jolt, off her lap, and ran out into the foyer.

CHAPTER SEVEN

THE DETECTIVE

OCTOBER 22, 2007

H annah woke up with a start. She immediately
began to think about Aunt Jewelia. The song she
was playing in her dream always made her feel mournful, although also comforted in a way. Actually being
in Jewelia's house had ignited in her a whole world
of curiosity about her aunt. And about herself—who
was she and why was she here? And who was Wixby?
She had never met a cat that could talk, despite often
wishing her childhood cat could speak. She may even
have had dreams that Mystera could speak. But this
dream was totally different. It seemed so plausible, so
real, so normal. She hadn't questioned it, realized it
was strange, or wondered what was going on while it
happened. It just was. It was as normal as any mundane
interaction in her daily life. But cats couldn't really
talk, right?

As her mind got clearer and she rolled out of bed,
she decided she should get something to drink to start
the day. She got up, picked out some fresh clothes from
her suitcase, and headed back down the hallway. She
passed the big window once again, except this time the

sun was out and she could see for the first time the vast
grandness of the pumpkin patch. The entire manor
was surrounded by it. It was the largest pumpkin patch
she had ever seen in her life. Her thoughts returned
immediately to her recurring dream.

Hannah suddenly got a feeling in her body, a shimmering tingle; her right ear started to ring and she felt
a flush of warm comfort pass over her. She almost felt
like tears arrived between her eyelashes, and her heart
lifted. But in a moment, the feeling was gone. Hannah
remained at the window, staring out across the patch
to the sea. She was meant to be here; she knew it now
in her bones.

Hannah headed down the stairs and down the
long hallway toward the kitchen. In the daylight, the
kitchen was magnificent. The ceiling soared to the
peaks of the manor, sun streaming down from above.
There were heavy wooden beams that crisscrossed it,
hanging lanterns suspended from them.

Hannah desperately wanted a warm tea. She spotted
an old kettle, filled it with water from the sink, and
reached for the clear glass vessel filled with tea bags.

As she sat sipping her tea, she thought again about
why her parents had not spoken to Jewelia for all those
years. What else did they have in common? What else
did she not know?

The sound of wind chimes outside roused her from
her thoughts and she looked out the large bay windows
in the kitchen. They offered an incredible view of the
grounds of the manor, and beyond to the sea in the
distance. A gentle breeze wafted in an open window
over the sink. As she gazed at the shore, she saw a
woman in the distance. Hannah could not make out her
face, but she could see that her hair was in a bun, she

had sunglasses on, and she was standing on the dock watching the coastal boats pass to and fro, searching the depths of the sea. Hannah's curiosity was peaked.

"Good Morning, Hannah! Are you finding everything okay?" Old Man Adams' face appeared at the window.

Hannah jumped. "Yes, thanks!" she replied, quickly recovering.

"Detective Norma Nyx showed up at my cottage this morning. She's leading the search for your aunt—I think she might have contacted you already? She'd like to speak with you, once you're ready."

"I'll be out in a few minutes." Hannah tried not to feel ruffled by the detective's reappearance. She grabbed a sweater she'd tossed over the chair and went out through the kitchen door to the backyard.

The woman with the bun had begun walking toward the manor and was nearly at the door when Hannah stepped out.

"Hello, Hannah. I didn't expect to see you in Maple Hollow, but glad you're here. I'd like to ask you a few questions, if I may."

"Okay." Hannah wasn't quite awake yet, but she had the sense there was something familiar about Norma. She couldn't quite place what it was.

Old Man Adams motioned to a gathering of patio chairs. "Let's all go sit over here," he said. They all sat down and Norma pulled out a notepad.

"Mr. Adams tells me you arrived yesterday on the island. Have you been to Maple Hollow before?"

"No, this is my first time," Hannah replied.

"How well do you know your Aunt Jewelia?"

"I've never met her in person, so I guess not very well. She used to send me cards and gifts growing up, but my parents weren't close with her, so..." Hannah trailed off.

"I see." Norma sat up stiffer in her chair, arching her spine. "And you had not heard from your aunt prior to her disappearance?"

Hannah shifted in her chair, trying not to mention the letter or the plane ticket. She was in the hot seat but, for some reason, didn't feel like revealing this strange piece of information. She also didn't like being cross-examined like she was a suspect. Old Man Adams looked similarly defensive. Perhaps he was worried that he was actually suspected in Jewelia's disappearance.

"When we spoke a few days ago, why did you not mention you were intending to travel here?" There it was—the question.

Hannah shifted in her chair again. "I...I didn't know I was coming, at that time. I decided after we talked that perhaps I should...should be here. That maybe I could help?"

"I see," Norma said again, peering at Hannah through the small glasses that rested on the edge of her nose. "How long do you plan to stay on the island?"

"She can stay as long as she wants," Old Man Adams chimed in, not letting Hannah answer.

Hannah smiled at him. She felt that Old Man Adams was attempting to deflect Norma's focus away from her.

"What are you doing to find Jewelia?" Old Man Adams added, his frustration beginning to boil over.

"We're doing everything we can," Norma replied. "I can't go into the details of this investigation, but we've got teams on the ground and in the water every day. If she's on the island, we'll find her." She stood up and held out her hand for Hannah to shake. "Thank you for your time. We may have additional questions as the investigation continues."

"I'll show you out," Old Man Adams said roughly.

He walked Norma to the front gate. Hannah could hear them speaking but could not tell what they were saying.

She heard the gate smack shut and saw Old Man Adams returning. He waved at Hannah and headed toward his cottage. She could tell he was worried.

Hannah resolved that she was not going to trust detectives or any authorities, this time or ever. She was going to have to investigate this herself. It was the only way she could find out the truth of what happened.

Once inside, she returned to her room, grabbed her phone, and sent a text to Maggie. "Hey," she wrote.

"Yeah?" was Maggie's quick reply. "Everything good?"

"Yes, there's so much going on, but I have to ask you something. Have you ever had a dream that just felt so real you weren't sure what to think?" she asked.

"Yeah, sometimes," Maggie replied.

"Have you ever wondered why we dream?" Hannah continued. Posing an existential question was not unusual for her, so she knew her roommate would not be stumped, even if it was by text.

"Not really," Maggie replied. Then Hannah waited, watching the three dots run across the screen.

"I don't think there's much to them," Maggie added, which only accentuated Hannah's internal vexation.

"I've always thought that dreams might be another world. It's weird we spend so much time there. There must be a greater reason, right?" she asked. "A few nights ago, I had this dream, it's kind of recurring but different."

"What's it about?" Maggie asked.

"I'm in this pumpkin patch, and vines begin to wrap around me, it feels like it's alive and part of me. I wake up feeling empowered and connected," Hannah typed.

"Wow, that sounds amazing," Maggie wrote. "I wish mine were like that. All I ever dream about is being chased. I always wake up right before I can get away or see who it is. I don't think dreams mean anything, they're just nonsense. I don't pay attention to mine, but if I did, I'd much rather have your dream."

"I just wish I knew what it meant," Hannah replied. "I've had it over the years, but never as strong as this time."

"I wouldn't put too much effort into trying to figure it out. Focus on why you're in Maple Hollow and stop spending so much time in your dreamworld," Maggie advised. "Let me know how you're getting on, okay? I worry about you."

"Thanks, I'll keep in touch." Hannah wondered if she should heed Maggie's advice, if she should just let things go and stop asking these questions about her dreams. Maybe her friend was right. Maybe they meant nothing.

CHAPTER EIGHT

THE HOLLOW

Hannah made herself a cup of warm tea. She pulled out the magazine from the plane to look at the photo of Aunt Jewelia, then began to read the accompanying article about the Halloween Hollow. It opened with an atmospheric musing:

> *In October, people in the northern hemisphere begin to turn their ears to the wind. Their breath mingles with the leaves that fall crackling to the ground. Their spirits quicken as they feel the shift: summer has waned, and fall is ushering itself in. It is an annual turning of the wheel, a process some dread and some welcome. But there is power in this passage. It is the harvest time. The time of year to embrace and celebrate the arrival of the coming winter. A time when the world becomes darker, yet richer in a more mysterious way.*
>
> *Autumn is unmistakably mystical. Fog rolls in, and the ground is dewy from moist rain. Leaves show their true colors as the chloro-*

*phyll drains from their veins. Fruits and veg-
etables burst in growth as the harvest nears.
Maple Hollow is no ordinary town. In fact, it
is quite extraordinary. It is in the soil, which
teams with it. It is in the air, which swirls with
it. It whispers in the bubbling brooks, sliding
through the forest. It is in the sparks popping
off the fire pits steeped in the darkness. People
are drawn to Maple Hollow from around the
world, all gathering to celebrate this sacred
time.*

Hannah wished it could always be fall. The transition to winter always came too quickly. She reflected on the article's mention of the leaves losing their
chlorophyll and showing their real colors. This meant
the leaves weren't actually "turning" at all; they were
merely becoming their true selves. Hannah liked that.
It meant that autumn, even though it was often viewed
as a season of decline heading toward inevitable cold
and darkness, was actually the most authentic time of
year. It was the way the world really was and should
be, without everything looking and being the same.
Without too much brightness or too much darkness. It
was the perfect in-between, and it was glorious. It was
meant to be appreciated.

She decided she was now ready to explore the rest
of the island. Perhaps if she could learn more about
what made Maple Hollow so extraordinary, her family history here, and her aunt's life, it could help her
discover what really happened. She pulled out the map
Old Man Adams had given her and traced the path she
would take. The sun was high in the sky as she rode the

bicycle into town. She hadn't caught much of a glimpse of Maple Hollow proper last night, since it was dark and raining when she arrived.

The town was small, with less than a dozen streets in total. All the leaves on all the trees were at peak color, some bursting with brilliant yellow, some deep orange, and still others a deep burgundy hue. As she rode, leaves drifted on the gentle breeze to the brick sidewalks, cascading down like a beautiful song.

She parked her bike and walked along the cozy tree-lined streets, charmed by what she saw. The buildings were old but well-kept. The streets were lined with black lamp posts, each bearing an enormous flower basket bursting with a myriad of colors. Orange and yellow mums were bountiful. She began to understand why her aunt had lived in Maple Hollow all her life—it was adorable. She also noticed how at home she felt here. It was as if she'd been here before. There was something that seemed so familiar, and so comforting. It felt right to be here, even though she wasn't sure why.

Leaves crunching beneath her feet, Hannah admired the shop windows. Each had its own unique version of Halloween displays and decorations, ready to welcome the upcoming festival-goers. Some were more on the whimsical side, golden-orange-themed arrangements with pumpkins and candy for the children. Others were darker-themed, with skulls, bones, and ghosts.

She thought about how this was the only time of year that people decorated with death. It was part of life, after all, an inevitable one, and one she knew all too well in her own life. Having been visited by death, and moving past it, Hannah knew she had a more profound appreciation of it then someone who had not had this experience. Despite all her darkness inside, she knew there was always light with the dark. That death was not the end; there was light on the other side of it. She had never believed that this life was all there was, that we only live once on Earth and nowhere else. It seemed ridiculous and almost pompous of anyone to assume that, and she wouldn't ever know enough to. Just because something cannot be seen with one's physical eyes does not mean it does not exist. Hannah was a seeker. She knew there was more, and she could not keep herself from looking for it.

That was part of why she came to Maple Hollow in the first place. She knew there was so much about her aunt she didn't know. She had been led here by some higher guidance she didn't quite understand yet. But she was beginning to hear whispers in her soul. Initially they had been so quiet and subtle she almost didn't notice them. But the more she tuned in, the more she connected with something greater than herself. She wasn't sure what it was or how she was doing it, but it was there.

As she came to a crosswalk, her eyes turned to the shop on the corner behind her. The display in its window was a combination of crystals, skeletons, and pumpkins, all sitting atop a bright orange tapestry. Nestled in between a pumpkin and a black lantern was a black cat. It was sleeping soundly as the sun shone through the glass window, warming its fur. Above the display on the window, etched in stained glass, were the words *Hollow is Home*. Reading it gave Hannah a rush of warmth. Tears suddenly began to well up in her eyes and again she had a tingling sensation that shimmered up her legs. Could Maple Hollow be her new home?

She put her hand on the door knob and crossed the threshold. It was a small metaphysical shop. The energy inside was amazing. Small tinkling sounds mixed with soothing ocean sounds, and a gentle melody echoed from a distance. It looked more like a cozy living room than a shop. There was a fire crackling in the fireplace on one wall. Surrounding the fireplace were thousands of books, jars, boxes, and the like.

"Welcome to Maple Moon," a woman's voice said slowly and confidently from the shadows. "And what is it you are seeking today?" she asked as she drew closer to Hannah. She wore a brilliant purple scarf that wrapped around her body and cascaded down into black velvet fringe. Her hair was silver, long, wild, and curly. Her eyes were the deep green of Ireland's cliffs.

"Hello," Hannah began. "I liked the sign in the window, so I thought I'd come in."

"Ah, there are signs everywhere, aren't there?" the woman said slowly. She reached out her hand to Hannah. "Pleased to meet you. I am Madame Morgan."

When Hannah's hand met hers, there was a tingle in her fingers. It was a spark of electricity, like a warm hug buzzing with life-force energy. They slowly shook hands.

"I'm Hannah. I'm—"

Before she could say anything further, Madame Morgan interrupted her. "You're Jewelia Skye's niece. Of course."

"Yes...how did you know?"

"There are no coincidences," Madame Morgan said, smiling mysteriously. "The universe aligns everything to happen at exactly the right time."

A gray cat appeared at the woman's ankles, rubbing its cheek on her skin and wrapping its tail around her leg. The light caught its fur, making it shimmer like an icy ocean of silver.

"And this is Merlin," she said, gently petting his head. "Oh, and the one sleeping up in the window is Milu. He's getting his afternoon sun. So, what can I help you with today, my dear?"

"I'm not exactly sure," Hannah began. "I came to Maple Hollow to help find my aunt. I just arrived last night. I thought I'd come into town to explore."

"Yes, of course! Explore, my dear." Madame Morgan waved her hand as if to say, don't mind me, take it all in. "I'll be back here if you need me." She nodded slightly and retreated toward the back of the shop, Merlin prancing happily behind her.

Hannah began to take in all the sights and smells of the shop. There was so much to look at. As she stood in front of a tall bookshelf filled to the brim, her ears perked to a distant call. It was Milu, walking from the front of the store toward her. In his mouth, he carried a soft cat toy shaped like a pumpkin. He was trying with all his might to get Hannah's attention, announcing the monumental delivery of his gift. Meowing loudly as he got closer, he dropped the pumpkin at her feet and gazed up knowingly at her with his seafoam eyes.

"Why thank you, Milu," Hannah exclaimed, picking up the pumpkin and patting him on the head. Satisfied at the acknowledgment, Milu turned and slowly sauntered back toward the front with the swagger of a wise jaguar tired from the hunt.

After perusing the shop a bit longer, Hannah remembered the task at hand. She tried to project her voice toward the back of the store: "Excuse me, Madame Morgan?"

"Yes, dear?" Morgan poked her head through the velvet curtains and re-entered the room.

"I...I'd like to ask you something." Hannah stared into the woman's knowing eyes.

"Of course you do, dear. Come sit down." Morgan raised her arms, inviting Hannah to join her at a table by the fire. "Can I get you something to drink?"

"Sure, I'd love some tea."

The table was small and flanked by two well-cushioned, comfortable-looking purple chairs. No sooner did Morgan sit than Merlin jumped into her lap to snuggle in. "He loves a warm lap," Morgan remarked as she placed an elegant teapot embossed with a sparkly moon emblem on the table, poured out the warm liquid into two small teacups, and passed one of them to Hannah.

Hannah gazed into the fire, watching the flames crackle and snap. Madame reached across the table, both her hands held out for Hannah's. "What is it you seek, my dear?"

"I've been having this dream," Hannah started.

"Ah dreams," Morgan exclaimed. "They are the portal to our souls." She spoke slowly and with a mystical tone. "Go on, dear, tell me your dream," she added quickly, realizing she'd interrupted.

Hannah began to tell her the dream, as best she could remember it. "I've had this dream since I was younger, many times. Sometimes there are slight differences but the main storyline is the same. It's fall, I'm in a pumpkin patch at nighttime, there's always a crescent moon in the sky, and the vines of the pumpkin patch wrap around me. I feel alive, with a life force that's magical and invigorating."

"I see." Morgan closed her eyes. She was still lightly holding Hannah's hands.

A silence passed over the room. The only sounds were the crackle of the fire and the slow purring of Merlin. Eventually Madame Morgan opened her eyes. She spoke slowly and succinctly.

"Pumpkins symbolize growth, positive change, and abundance coming into your life. They represent a transition. For something to begin, sometimes, something else must end. It is the cycle of life. Sometimes positive change is born out of negativity. It's the dark before the light." She paused, then looked directly into Hannah's eyes. "Embrace this new change, my dear."

Hannah felt a chill rise up her thighs, to her back, and up into her neck. It went straight to her head and tingled like she'd just plunged into a cold pool.

Morgan's gaze drifted again. "The moon in your dream is the darkness of your soul. It is beckoning you to discover, to unearth your darkness. The crescent moon is the beginning, or the end—it is the end of one phase and the beginning of another. Lastly, my dear, the vines are your spiritual inheritance." Then she gently let go of Hannah's hands, putting them together and patting them on top.

Hannah sat still, feeling enveloped, as if surrounded by a warm island breeze. Her heart felt full and calm. Tears peeked out of the corners of her eyes.

"Wow, thank you," she said. "I've...never felt this way before."

"You are at the beginning, dear, but you are moving fast. I have a sense it will all be revealed soon." At that, Merlin leaped from Morgan's lap and she rose from her chair. "Please come see me again, dear."

"Yes, I most surely will. Thank you again." Hannah also rose.

Morgan gave her a knowing look, as if to silently part as souls. A slight smile on her face, a glow of kindness.

Hannah smiled back, nodding in acknowledgment.

Madame Morgan slowly returned to the back of the store, the velvet curtains closing behind her. Merlin followed, his tail the last thing Hannah could see as it curled into a question mark between the curtains.

Chapter Nine

THE LANTERN

Oct 3, 2007

A bright light flashed through the window, the thunder crashing and rolling far away. The parlor was still except for the sound of the rain steadily tapping on the window. The window took up the majority of the wall, framed by a dark purple half-moon top with columns on each side. Each windowpane was separated with wrought iron. The top rows of each window were filled with a triangular shape that glowed red when the lightning flashed. The floor was a purplish-gray wood. The sitting area was framed by red curtains hung from the ceiling, long on either side and draped along the top. Antique chairs with elegantly rounded backs and Queen Anne-type feet surrounded the grand piano, which sat in the center. A candelabra was on top, with nine candles, each one with a golden flame.

Cobwebs graced the corners of the large window, glowing white in the moonlight. Jewelia was often too engrossed in her work to worry about mundane things such as dusting, or even sometimes eating. She was completely and unflinchingly focused on her inner world. She had always dreamed, as long as she could remember. But recently her dreams had stopped. She would wake up with no recollection, no message, no comforting guidance or warning, just silence. She had a bad feeling something nefarious was at work. Something was preventing her dreams. She feared the worst.

She sat on the piano bench, staring out the window. Sometimes closing her eyes. Not playing, just listening. She was listening to the silence between the raindrops. Listening to the spirits around her to help her solve this riddle and lead her in the right direction.

She had been told when she was younger that it was a bad omen if your dreams stopped. She'd heard rumors of others whose mission it was to stop dreams. They did not mean well. Because of this knowledge, she had always paid attention to her dreams. But now, there weren't any, and she knew something was wrong.

She thought about Mercury retrograde and how it can disrupt energy and skew the spiritual fields, allowing nefarious spirits who otherwise were held back to hold sway. She wondered if this was what was at play. A foreboding feeling filled her chest.

She heard footsteps out in the foyer, slow and steady on the stairs. Then it stopped. She didn't turn to look. Midnight was sleeping soundly in the chair next to her, so she knew it wasn't him. Then a glowing light appeared in the windowpane. It was not outside.

As she fixed her eyes on the window, the light began to move across the entrance to the parlor behind her. It appeared like a floating shadow of a person carrying a lantern. The apparition stopped near one of the columns. Jewelia slowly turned her head to look behind her, but when her gaze finally made it around, there was nothing there. She looked back to the window, but again, no glowing light.

Was someone trying to contact her or trying to access her thoughts? Was it someone in need of help? Was it a family spirit coming to help her? Or was it those she'd been warned about, those who were causing her dreams to stop? Thoughts raced through her head. She knew she might be in danger, and knew she must do something to prevent it.

Chapter Ten

THE PASSAGE

Oct 12, 2007

Although Jewelia was an eccentric, she wasn't exactly a recluse. She would dine occasionally at a small spot called the Dishwasher Café. It was a quaint bistro, right on the main street in town, that was always bustling. But she ordered that night in a hurry. She didn't exactly feel like lingering, so she asked for her order to go. She stood in the entrance of the café and spoke quietly to the hostess, who was half-listening to her, half-checking her phone.

When her food was ready, a man brought it out from the back. He was tall, definitely over six feet. His forearms were large, sleeves rolled up to his elbows exposing dark tattoos all over his skin as he passed the bag to Jewelia. He had a wiry red beard, a broad chest, and the stature and manner of a sailor.

With her order in hand, Jewelia scurried back to her car. It was raining again and she didn't want the flimsy brown paper bag to get soaked and fall apart before she could make it back home.

Back at the manor, upon taking her last bite, she began to feel extraordinarily tired. Her head felt heavy and her upper-body muscles weak, like she'd sat in a hot bath for too long. She disposed of the to-go wrappers in the trash, left the fire burning, and headed up to lie down in her bed. She fell into a deep, deep stupor of a sleep that really wasn't a sleep at all.

***

Outside, clouds raced past the moon as the sky whirled in the stormy night. Detective Norma Nyx stood motionless under a thick maple tree. She listened to the bare tree branches scratching at the floor-to-ceiling windows that looked out to the water. The library at Skye Manor was built to sit right out on the shore. Norma knew this side of the manor was more isolated and it would be easy to slip inside unseen through an open window.

Bookshelves lined the walls from ceiling to floor, on which there were countless volumes stacked in different directions. The only light in the room came from the fireplace, the glow of the flames still crackling. The moonlight illuminated a large landscape painting in a gilded frame sitting atop the mantle. A large, wide-brimmed black hat hung on a coat hook near the fire. Below it was a cloak, and below that were boots, still wet from the rain. Two burgundy velvet chairs sat in front of a large window. In front of them was a small wooden desk. On top was a teapot, an empty cup of tea, a stack of books, and one open book on a stand. Below the desk, a vintage plum, black, and white Persian rug covered the bare wood floor.

Now that Jewelia was out cold, Norma silently poked around in the library. She was looking for a key, but not just any key. She needed to find the fabled key of Skye Manor.

Her creeping footsteps broke the silence in the otherwise quiet room. She stood in front of the tall bookcases and began to gently tug on each book spine, checking to see if it was in fact a real book or perhaps a fake book meant to obscure something. She boldly continued to turn over items on the desk, and even sifted through the cloak and the boots.

After a long time of searching, Norma noticed a slight discoloration in the wood of the bookshelves. As she ran her fingers across it, she could feel there was an alteration, a bump. She shined her mini-flashlight on the shelf. There were two books that appeared almost stuck together—they didn't easily give in to her fingers when she attempted to pull them apart. She started pulling harder and harder on the books, but they would not move; it was as if they were glued to the bookshelf. She shifted her weight and attempted to force the books toward her. Then she heard it—a creak underneath her feet. She shifted her weight again, and again she heard a creak. For leverage, she put her full weight on one foot on the creaky floorboard and both hands on the two books. The floorboard was connected to the books. When pressing her weight into the board, the books began to lean forward. Then suddenly, the entire bookcase next to that one popped open with a creak.

It was a secret passageway. She slid into the darkness.

CHAPTER ELEVEN

THE GIFT

OCTOBER 22, 2007

While getting ready for bed that night, Hannah's frustration grew as she found herself continually staring at Aunt Jewelia's letter. She thought about her interaction with Madame Morgan. The words "darkness of your soul" echoed in her mind. Morgan had also said, "it is beckoning you to discover, to unearth your darkness." Hannah was ruminating on those words. What was her darkness? What was waiting for her to discover?

While brushing her hair and staring at her reflection in the mirror, she started to think about the disconnect she felt with the world. Well, not the whole world, just certain parts of it, such as other people. Hannah preferred animals to people. She loved a good conversation, but that wasn't the point. Conversations didn't always have words, and most people didn't understand that. Or if they did, the conversations were never about the words that were spoken. Energy followed people and surrounded them like light or shadow. It was unavoidable and part of the dance. She didn't always feel like having a dance partner.

For this reason, among so many others, she'd always felt more at home among animals. It wasn't so much that they needed her, more that they needed someone to understand. When all those things were lost in translation, for others, she could hear. But it wasn't like normal hearing. In fact, it had very little to do with her ears at all. It was her heart, her mind, her soul, all at the same time. Agreeing to listen, agreeing to understand, even though the language wasn't the same. It didn't have to be.

She only liked surrounding herself with people she felt could understand that. But she never actually discussed it. Of course, it wouldn't need to be discussed if it was truly understood. Those who knew, didn't say, and those who said, didn't know. There had come a time when those around her, like Maggie, tried to convince her the world just wasn't this way, that pursuing this way of thinking was misleading at best. It only made her want to be around people less.

Hannah had always believed she could see through the mundane world everyone else held so close, where they found safety in normative, routine expectedness. She always felt there was something else, right there in the midst of all of it, overlooked by those who preferred to pass by, unacknowledged by those who claimed to have examined it, and, worst of all, covered up or denied by those who may have unwittingly stumbled upon it.

There once was a time she didn't feel this way. She had subscribed to different philosophies along the way, but they never really synced with everything she felt. She held tight to the idea that someday, the true explanation for her sense of knowing unease would reveal itself. Perhaps this was what Madame Morgan meant, perhaps it was time for her knowing to reveal itself. Perhaps it really was time to "unearth her darkness."

Who was she, really? Who was she supposed to be? She tried to disguise herself, sometimes, so she would appear to blend in with normal society, but it never really worked. Not everyone could appreciate her true nature. Or maybe it was she herself that didn't? She was always more serious than everyone else; something made her feel that she was not quite as unburdened as everyone prancing about laughing at everything all the time. It seemed like she'd go days or longer never laughing. As if a heavy dark cloud was always following her around, rather than the radiant sunshine bursting overhead, making everything clear and bright.

She considered herself an old soul.

There were some people who looked, from the outside, like maybe they felt like she did on the inside, but it turned out to be superficial and they actually weren't as dark as they appeared. She, on the other hand, felt very dark on the inside and didn't look so dark on the outside. This confused people. They would think she should be cheery when she wasn't. Or that her life must be simple like theirs, when it wasn't. Or that she never had dark thoughts or feelings, which she did. Feelings she couldn't share with anyone. Feelings she'd held up inside and buried deep within her, since no one would understand them anyway.

Always feeling so deep and dark was a familiar cavern for Hannah, one she'd fallen down many times and nearly lost herself in. It was as if she was sitting at the bottom of a hole, peering up at a shimmering light way out of reach, which cast thin rays of light that tried to reach her. But she was deep in the shadows, trying to find her way back up. Carefully choosing which mask to wear, which person she'd try to be. Anyone but herself.

Hannah loved thunderstorms, the sound of crickets, the warmth of the sun on the back of her legs, when the wind would pick up a curl of her hair. The soothing greeting of a gently waving tree in the breeze, and the solemn yet blazing evening when the final stretches of light grabbed all that was left and splattered it across the sky in a brief yet spectacular sendoff, before starting all over again. She savored the crunch of fallen leaves below her feet, the stiffness of the hairs in her nose on a chill day, and most importantly the utter rapture of mystery she felt when surrounded by fog, no matter the time of day.

All of these things were real at the manor. They all made sense, welcomed her, and comforted her. For these reasons and more, she felt connected here, like it was where she was always supposed to be.

She'd felt this before when she was very young. When she would be in nature. It was alive, buzzing, and she was part of it. Communing but never really speaking, she was part of this world and at the same time beyond it. Or maybe it just was beyond what anyone would accept, condone, admit. It didn't matter; it was a part of her, just as much as her fingernails, the protein strands of her hair, and the breath in her lungs. To her it was real, and it didn't matter what anyone else thought. She valued her oft-criticized idealism, her hopeful soft heart, her longing for connection that wasn't synced, wasn't matched, couldn't be communicated in all the ways science said it must.

Madame Morgan had told her to "embrace this new change." Hannah's thoughts traced back once more to her pumpkin patch dream and what Morgan had said about pumpkins representing transition. "Sometimes positive change is born out of negativity." There must be a reason she was here. She had lost her job—that was the negativity—and she had always felt disconnected, lost and dark. That was negativity too. But where was the positive change? What was she transitioning to? Where was the light from her darkness? What was her spiritual inheritance?

"It's the dark before the light." Madame Morgan's words echoed in her head. Hannah's eyes became heavy as she repeated this phrase over and over in her head as she slowly drifted off to sleep.

Hannah found herself walking alone, late at night, down a long empty street lined with tall trees. At the end of the street, she saw her Aunt Jewelia's manor. She was in a hurry and felt a bit frantic to get there. She was walking at a steady pace, but the more she walked, the more it seemed like she wasn't going anywhere. And her legs felt heavy and not functioning right. It was as if she had to keep sliding along. She'd take one step with her right foot, then slide her left like she was on ice skates. Then another step with her left, and sliding along with her right.

A feeling of frustration began to grow inside her. Why was it taking so long to get there? And why was she having such difficulty? As she watched the manor off in the distance, the street began to bend and turn, and then she would lose sight of it and pump her legs harder. It was as if she was on a loop and with each distance gained, more distance was introduced between herself and the manor.

On her back was a backpack, heavy and filled with books. She hadn't actually looked at the books, but she instinctively knew they were the source of the weight on her shoulders. She also didn't know why she was carrying them around, but apparently she was supposed to bring them with her.

Eventually she decided to take off the backpack. She pulled on the scratchy straps digging into her shoulders. First one side, then the other. She hurled the backpack off to the right. She wasn't sure if it landed anywhere or just dissolved. At that moment, she somehow zoomed forward to the front of the manor. The manor was lit up brightly, all the outside lights glowing like an undersea castle. She could hear distant voices of the people inside, but could not make out what they were saying.

When she got close to the main entry, she could see the outline of a fluffy figure near the worn wooden steps. It was Wixby. He sat like a regal statue saluting a queen, his glowing aquamarine eyes looking straight into her gaze. Hannah stopped, not sure if Wixby was going to attempt to stop her or was there to greet her.

"Sometimes we need only ask for a direction to find one," Wixby intoned in his high-pitched yet confident lisp.

The wind was beginning to blow harder. A big gust slammed into the manor door, blowing it open. Hannah stepped inside. "I'm going to do this my way," she said defiantly.

"I wouldn't have it any other way," Wixby said from behind her, in a very matter-of-fact, unsurprised manner.

CHAPTER TWELVE

THE LIBRARY
OCTOBER 23, 2007

T he next morning, Hannah jolted awake to a loud
knocking on the front door. She made her way
down the long staircase while tightening her ponytail.
The sun glistened through the stained glass in the
foyer, casting a kaleidoscope of swirling patterns on
the floor.

"Well, hello little lady! Just seeing how you are coming along," Old Man Adams said to her as she opened
the door.

"Oh, hi," she said, feeling relieved. "Please come in!"
She stepped aside so he could enter the foyer. Without
waiting for Adams to ask any questions or bothering
with casual small talk, she asked abruptly, "What can
you tell me about my father's relationship with my
aunt?"

Adams looked surprised but nodded. "Well, all I can
say is that he kept his distance from his sister once he
left the family manor. He chose to leave when he met
your mother. I guess he wanted to make his own way.
Like any siblings, they had their differences. Jewelia
never had children and never left."

Hannah had a hard time believing that was all there was to it. Was there something else her father was distancing himself from? "Was Aunt Jewelia sick before she disappeared?"

Adams' eyes widened as he looked at her, searching for how he should answer. "Yes," he said, looking now into the parlor with a defeated expression on his face. "She was...there was something not right about her. I can't say exactly what. In the weeks before the storm, she was increasingly stressed. Rather frantic. Every day she spent a lot of time alone with her books. All hours of the night, too—I could see her through the windows when I checked the grounds, spilling over her books by candlelight to no end. I did try to talk to her, but she seemed inconsolable. Driven, in a way I'd never seen her before, yet taxed like she was struggling with something she couldn't control."

Hannah almost held her breath, her thoughts running faster than Old Man Adams' words, only able to gather every fourth phrase or so. She was thinking about Jewelia's letter. Although she got the general sentiment of what Adams was saying, she wouldn't be able to exactly repeat it, being too engrossed in her perplexing thoughts. "So, what happened that night?" she asked directly. "The night Aunt Jewelia disappeared."

Adams sighed. "There was a terrible storm, a hurricane technically. The manor grounds suffered a lot of damage, as did much of the island. For some reason I'll never understand, Jewelia went out on the rowboat. It was a fool's errand in that weather, though. She never should have gone near the water! The winds were too high and the tides had swelled to dangerous levels, as if the lightning and thunder weren't warning enough of a peril." He stopped, wiped his brow, and stared at the floor.

Hannah, realizing how upset Adams was, stayed silent and continued to listen.

"I saw her from my kitchen window as she ran toward the dock," he went on. "I ran out after her, but she was too quick and determined. She got in the boat and was out on the water by the time I made it to the dock. I yelled after her, but she probably couldn't hear me over the storm."

He moved to sit on a Victorian bench in the foyer. His fingers paced over the roped edging.

"She never came back to shore. Her boat was never found. Even though it is a missing person's case at the moment, I think the authorities are basically filing her in their 'lost at sea' category. But it just doesn't add up to me. I know it's possible for people to be lost at sea, and it happens all the time, yet I have this feeling I can't shake about it. It's unsettling. Sometimes I feel like Jewelia is still here."

"I understand," Hannah said. She was careful to not say *I'm so sorry*, although she wanted to extend her sympathy for his grief. "I wonder why she would go out on the water in a hurricane, putting herself in danger that way. I'm still trying to figure out how to read her letter."

"Have you been to her library?" Old Man Adams asked. "Jewelia spent all her time there. The entrance is under the staircase," he added as Hannah stared at him, confused. He stood up and put his hand on the door. "Also, you might want to talk to Miss Ashlin Aldona, keeper of all the history of the island at the library in town. She may be able to help. It looks like the authorities are scanning the sea again today, looking for any signs of Jewelia. I'm going to go feed Midnight. Let me know if you need anything."

"Okay, thank you. I will do that," Hannah said as they parted ways.

After Adams left, she walked over to the small door underneath the stairs. It was quite unremarkable at first glance, and almost hidden if you didn't walk over to it.

She stared closely at the door. The knotty pine of the wood panels held spiral memories of faces, each circle holding a familiar etching she'd felt she'd long forgotten. One was the silhouette of a woman, her eyelash drooping down, long hair swirling about, with open lips. Another was a dog's face, with taut ears and long nose. And something that looked to Hannah like a dragon or something supernatural, flying into the clouds.

As she pushed open the door, it creaked and became caught on a rug on the floor. She squeezed past and followed a short hallway that turned sharply to the right. Within moments, she had entered the most fantastical and magical library she had ever seen. On either side, each wall was filled with books. From ceiling to floor were books, every shelf crammed. The bookcases must have each had eight or more levels. Hannah took a deep breath and savored the nostalgic scent only aged books can bear, mixed with wax and notes of incense.

Some shelves held small frames scattered among the books. They displayed faded brown-and-white photos of family members from the past, mostly taken in fields or in front of Skye Manor. Some shelves were lined with a luxurious velvet of burnished jewel tones; some also had trinkets that bore unusual symbols, placed next to spare candles of deep colors. Each book seemed to glow with a rich saturation, in a way that made the entire room feel like a treasure trove. The tops of the shelves curved in large arches into a ceiling that was anything but flat and ordinary. It was magical—the ceiling looked like the bottom of the ocean, swirled with small ridges, hills and dales, turquoise and green, mixed with earthly bronze colors. Small candles were scattered about everywhere, many partially melted at different phases of having been lit. As Hannah drew closer to one of the bookcases, she began to see that each book had its own color scheme, with a unique scene painted on the spine.

She pulled a book off a shelf and started to flip through the pages. *The Art of Reversal Magick* was the title on the cover, in a large script font. She scanned some of the pages and read a few paragraphs: *The Art of Reversal is one that should not be attempted except in extreme cases of duress. Adequate steps of preparation and precaution should always be taken before beginning any reversal magick.*

Magick? Was her aunt truly into magick? Was that why her parents never mentioned Jewelia that much?

And was that why Jewelia had mysteriously disappeared?

Hannah set the book down and fished for another. *Mercury Retrograde Compendium.* Flipping open to a page, she read:

> *Mercury retrograde is a celestial event that happens several times per year, and lasts for a three-week period. During this time, it appears as if the planet of Mercury is moving backward, although it is not. This move-*

ment of the planets can have a great ef-
fect on those on earth. It can cause electri-
cal disturbances, miscommunications, delays,
and other energetic conflicts. Each retrograde
contains three phases: pre-retrograde, retro-
grade, and post-retrograde. The two weeks be-
fore and after retrograde are shadow periods
known as retroshade, when residual effects
of the stronger middle phase can be expe-
rienced. Each retrograde can have different
effects on people depending on their astro-
logical chart. Some may experience very emo-
tional and searching times, while others may
simply encounter a series of uncanny incon-
veniences.

"Fascinating," Hanna said aloud. She wondered how
often it happened. She flipped to the back of the book
and found an almanac of dates showing each year and
the retrograde periods for Mercury.

Her eyes zeroed in on this year, 2007.

Feb 14–March 8
Jun 15–July 10
Oct 12–Nov 1 (Pre-Retroshade Sept 21 - Oct
12)

October 12 through November 1! That was now! It
was Mercury retrograde right now! And Jewelia had
disappeared on Oct 12, the first day of retrograde.
Hannah began to put the pieces together. No wonder
her flight had been delayed. No wonder the radio in

Old Man Adams' car was acting up. Perhaps even losing her job was all because of retrograde.

What if her aunt's disappearance had something to do with Mercury retrograde? What if she had attempted some sort of reversal magick and it had gone awry? This new information confirmed Hannah's gut feeling that there was more to uncover.

She looked again at the book. This retrograde period was set to end on Nov 1, which was only a week away. She must find a way to discover what happened to Jewelia and to reverse it before retrograde was over. In fact, that meant she had to find her by Halloween night. She had eight days left.

Hannah ran back to the kitchen and began rummaging through the drawers looking for some tape. Then she sprinted upstairs to her room and grabbed Aunt Jewelia's letter. She taped it to the wall next to the bed.

She was going to figure out what the letter said if it meant the end of her. There had to be some explanation for why she couldn't read it, and maybe if she forced herself to look at it all the time she'd figure it out. Maybe she should get out of her head, see things from a different perspective. She decided to call Maggie to bounce some ideas around.

"Hey, how have you been?" she asked as soon as Maggie picked up the phone.

"Fine, how about you?" Maggie replied cheerily. "How's it going in Maple Hollow?"

"I'm not sure," Hannah said with some hesitation. She stared at the letter on the wall. "It's okay so far. I mean, everyone is nice enough, but I still haven't figured out the meaning of the letter."

"What letter?" Maggie asked. Hannah realized she had been in such a hurry to get to the island that she'd never mentioned the letter, and how strange it was, to Maggie.

"Oh, that's part of the reason I came. As well as that call from the detective. I got a letter from my aunt that she must have written before she disappeared. The problem is, I can't read it."

"You can't read it?" Maggie was confused. "As in, you can't bring yourself to read it, or you don't understand what it says?"

"It's not legible," Hannah explained. "Like it's in a foreign language or some weird code."

"Oh. Well, did you ask anyone else in the town if they knew what happened to your aunt?"

"Yes, but apparently Jewelia was very private about things, so I haven't learned anything. I'm going to the local library today to ask around."

"Can you send me a picture of the letter, so I can check it out?" Maggie asked.

"Yeah, sure, I can do that."

Hannah stood up and walked over to where the letter hung on the wall. She held up her phone and snapped a picture, then hit send.

"Okay, just sent."

"Okay cool, I'll check it out. Listen, I have to run to work, sorry!"

"Thanks, I'll talk to you later." Hannah hung up.

She had always looked to Maggie as a voice of reason, someone very grounded in reality. Maggie didn't believe anything until she could see it with her own eyes and it could be proven scientifically. Hannah knew this helped her friend feel safe, but in her opinion, she felt it blocked her off from the rest of existence which she was missing.

She pulled up the image of the letter on her phone, then looked back and forth between the phone and the actual letter on the wall. She crept up to the letter and ran her fingers across the ink.

What was Aunt Jewelia trying to tell her? Did this letter explain her disappearance? Did it tell her something that, as the last remaining family member, she needed to know? Why did Old Man Adams not know what it was? Were there other letters, perhaps with other messages, hidden somewhere in the manor?

***

Hannah spent the rest of the afternoon exploring the manor looking for other clues. There were so many rooms, each with its own mysteries. As Hannah ate dinner that night, sitting on the hard wooden chair in the kitchen, she suddenly had another flashback to that morning she'd gotten the news about her parents. Her boney behind pressing into the unforgiving wooden chair, her spine pressed against the back slats, all of it making her feel awkward and wrong. She remembered wanting to escape—to disappear. Remembering this moment brought back all the feelings of disconnection, of loss, of feeling lost. She didn't want to relive that again. She couldn't bear the thought of not finding Aunt Jewelia, of losing her from her life. She hadn't even *had* her in her life, of course, but the thought of losing another connection was almost too much to bear.

She thought again about what she had discovered about Mercury retrograde. What role did retrograde play? She wasn't finding any answers despite her best efforts. How was she supposed to integrate the retrograde information into discovering what had happened? And what was going to happen once retrograde was over? Was it a period that made things possible, or screwed things up, or both?

As she sat quietly in the kitchen, there was no sound besides the distant ticking of a clock. She shuffled her feet impatiently as that feeling rose again that she must do something. She felt more compelled than ever to dive headfirst into this mystery. To immerse herself in the dark shadows of what may lie beyond. As cryptic and inscrutable as the situation appeared, she innately also knew that inside her there was an answer, if she could only find it. In her head the line echoed from one of the books: *Some may experience very emotional searching times.* This was such a time. She felt compelled and yet so lost; how was it possible to hold these two feelings together at the same time? Perhaps she was compelled to become lost? To lose herself in a surrender to the mystery? Maybe she had to let go of something to find something.

Hannah no longer felt hungry. In fact, eating was the furthest thing from her mind. She pulled away from the table and walked slowly back up to her bedroom. From the hallway, she could see where the letter was taped to the bedroom wall.

She stood still for a moment, thinking perhaps standing far away from it might cause something to be revealed, something that wasn't obvious if one was too close. She tried squeezing her eyes, squinting at first, then moved from side to side, looking at the letter from each angular perspective. But it looked the same, and she remained confused and frustrated. She realized she must think outside the box.

Hannah sat on her bed, grabbed her journal, and began to write all her frustrations down. The words poured out of her like water flowing down a municipal drain after a storm. So much dark water. She wrote and wrote until her hand began to cramp under the strain of keeping up with her racing mind. Purged of her frustrations, she finally rested her head on the pillow and drifted off to sleep.

S teady rain fell on the craggy rocks below. Lightning pulsed in the sky, illuminating the thick gray clouds from within.

Ocean waters met the shoreline and mingled among the large rocks. Each new wave raced to the shore, foam building on top, the wave gently tumbling, sometimes peaking in the center, then dissipating into a foggy cloud and crashing into the rocks.

Hannah was sitting on a large rock looking out to the dark ocean. She felt discouraged. Her bones shivered in the icy air, her jacket drenched from the unrelenting rain. She reached her right hand into her pocket and her fingers traced the edges of a circular object. As she pulled it out, she noticed it was a compass—an antique compass.

A slow, steady beam from the lighthouse swept to and fro, piercing the darkness.

Hannah held the compass up to the light. It was tarnished from age, but she could tell it was once a shiny gold. On the front there was an engraving of a skeleton key.

She opened the compass and watched as the arrows inside spun around erratically, at first fast and frantic, then slowly, like a pendulum led by a heavy hand.

Her eyes became fixed on the compass—watching, waiting.

The rain continued to fall. The lighthouse beam paced over her, casting an intermittent glow on her shadow. Then the rain suddenly stopped and the water calmed.

Hannah looked out to the water. Stars began to illuminate the sky, twinkling in the deep darkness. As she stared at the horizon, out of the water came glowing lights. There were paper lanterns emerging from the water. There were thousands of them.

The sounds of distant piano music filled the air. Hannah didn't recognize the song, but it was the most beautiful, soothing piano music she'd ever heard.

Each lantern was rising at a different speed, but all were moving gracefully out of the glassy depths. There was no wind. The lanterns moved as if it was all planned. They knew where they were going, and they were surrendering to the air. As they rose, a golden glow emanated from the center of each lantern, turning them a harvest orange on top. Their shapes were slightly tapered near the bottom, where the glow was a pure white.

The lanterns were so light; their paper construction enabled them to rise up with just enough substance to catch the air. The glow of the lanterns reflected on the water, the gentle ripples spreading the glow. As she watched the lanterns continue to rise and float into the sky, Hannah looked up and felt hopeful. It was as if each lantern represented something positive that could happen, and there were so many, it meant the possibilities were endless. As they departed the water, they were effortless in their ascension.

As Hannah thought how beautiful it was, a feeling of peace came over her. She sat and watched the lanterns for what seemed like a long time. It was as if time had stopped. She didn't want to leave this place. She wanted to dwell here. It was comforting, beautiful and inspiring. She felt filled with hope in a way she couldn't remember ever feeling before. The lantern glow soothed her soul, becoming an energy of love that filled her from the inside. It was as if the lanterns were telling her everything was going to be okay, that she could let go and let her feelings and worries rise up. That she could rise above her fears, if only she let the natural forces of life release her. If only she surrendered to letting go.

CHAPTER THIRTEEN

THE LETTER

OCT 24, 2007

H annah awoke the next morning with a start. It was still before dawn, thick overcast skies obscuring the morning light. She thought she heard music, but then figured it must have been part of her dream. It turned out it was Midnight. He was making a loud meowing noise and carrying something in his mouth. He dropped a single match at Hannah's feet and flapped his tail proudly, staring into her soul.

"Oh, hello Midnight, what did you bring me? A match?" She looked at him inquisitively, bending over to pet his head.

As she stood up, holding the match in her hand, her eyes were drawn to the letter on the wall. Inspiration struck. She grabbed an iron candlestick from the dresser and lit the match. A hiss and spark ignited, and then a single plume of smoke rose into the air. She scurried over to the letter, snatched it off the wall, and hurried over to the mirror, waving the candlelight behind the letter. There she stood, gazing into the mirror and holding the letter in her hands, much like

Old Man Adams had stood perplexed at the airport waiting for her arrival.

The incomprehensible writing on the letter began to swirl and move as her pupils attempted to focus. At first her eyes became heavy, a veil of blurry tension overcoming them, but then everything suddenly became clear. As she looked at the letter in the mirror, illuminated by the candlelight, she could read it.

Dear Hannah,

If you are reading this, then what I feared most has already taken place. I hoped to never send you this letter, but the time has come that I must break the silence. It is time for you to know the truth about us. We are not like everyone else. Our families crossed the oceans many moons ago, drawn to this island.

The women in Maple Hollow are part of a secret society, a legacy of magick. We can travel to other dimensions and we each have special powers. I know this might seem crazy, but it's true. You are part of this legacy. Some call us witches, healers or guides.

We are the Healers of the Hollow. There are others, they are not like us, and they have a different intent. Some of them are called the Dream Haunters. They track people's dreams and trap them in their nightmares. For generations the families of Maple Hollow have battled dark forces such as the Dream Haunters. It has been hundreds of years since anything has happened, but in the last few weeks, since the equinox, I sense a shift.

I have ceased to dream, and I realize now it is because of the Dream Haunters. This can only mean one thing. They are back, and they are going to trap me. My attempt to reverse their power has failed thus far. I don't have much time left. They are coming. The veil is thinning, Halloween is near.

If you are reading this, it is because I am trapped. Trapped in an eternal nightmare by the Dream Haunters. Retrograde has weakened me and em-powered them. You must stop them before Halloween ends.

Discover the key. Open the portal. Save our legacy.

You now are my only hope.

Love,

Aunt Jewelia

What was Aunt Jewelia talking about? Who were the Dream Haunters? And what was the portal? Was Jewelia referring to the keys to the manor that Old Man Adams had given her when she arrived? Hannah's mind whirled with possible scenarios. How come she had never heard about any of this before? How did her family have a lineage she had never been told anything about?

Perhaps if she found out more about the manor, its history and her family history, it would help her free Jewelia. If only her parents were still alive to fill in the gaps. And she needed to find out exactly what happened the night Jewelia disappeared.

Hannah set the letter on the dresser and quickly called Maggie. "I figured it out!" she said the moment her friend answered. "Well sort of," she continued. "I don't know what it means, but I figured out how to read the letter! I lit a match that Midnight brought me—he's a cat—and then the letter revealed itself in the mirror!"

"Wait, a cat brought you what? And you saw what in the mirror?" Maggie was bewildered.

"I lit a candle with the match Midnight brought me, and I held it up behind the letter in the mirror," Hannah explained.

"Oh, that's odd," Maggie said.

"I get the feeling I don't know the whole story, but I think I might know what happened to Aunt Jewelia," Hannah told her breathlessly.

"What do you mean?"

"I don't know, but I better find out quickly!" Hannah was thinking out loud.

"This sounds dangerous." Maggie sounded concerned this time.

"I have to figure out what to do." Hannah's hands had begun to sweat and there was a feeling of tightness in her chest. "The letter tells me why Jewelia wanted me to come here. I have to find her, before Halloween."

"Just please be careful," Maggie said. "I worry about you being there by yourself."

"Oh, I'm not alone," Hannah assured her. "There's the caretaker, Old Man Adams. He lives on the property. In fact, I think that's who I'll talk to first about this."

Hannah said goodbye to Maggie and quickly called Old Man Adams to tell him she was finally able to read Jewelia's letter.

"What did it say?" he asked with concern.

Hannah quickly summarized the contents. "And she said...they are coming here. Any idea who these Dream Haunters would be?"

"Coming here?" he asked, still confused. "Coming here for what?"

"She says these forces have been after our family for years, and she was expecting them to trap or kidnap her. My guess is she tried to avoid them by going out on the water, but they must have gotten to her. She said something about a portal, and I found a book in her library that said Mercury retrograde is a planetary event happening right now. It ends on Halloween. I'm not sure what it all means, but she said I was her only hope."

"So, Jewelia was kidnapped?" Old Man Adams was still trying to wrap his head around it.

"It sounds like it. It sounds very serious, and we don't have much time left."

"Should we tell the detective?"

"I still don't have a good feeling about that," Hannah said. "Maybe Jewelia left behind some more information? I'll head to the library in town today to see Ashlin Aldona. I'll call you later."

Chapter Fourteen

THE OTHERWORLD

H annah rode her bike to town, heading for the Maple Hollow library. What was Halloween, anyway? She had grown up like so many other people, celebrating the holiday the way children do, dressing up in costumes and trick-or-treating for candy. But Hannah knew that not everyone did that, and that there were many countries and millions of people in the world that maybe didn't even know what Halloween was like. She had to uncover things that probably her aunt already knew, and maybe it would help her understand what happened to her.

The autumnal scenes she passed along the way, while nostalgically beautiful, felt poignant in her heart. On front lawns, children leapt into large piles of leaves raked up by their watchful parents. They delighted in the crunching sound, the earthy smell, the golden colors, and the fantastical experience of being able to dive in and through the massive mounds, toppling their parents' work. It took Hannah back to when she was younger, and her own parents, before that dark shadow eclipsed her youthful innocence. A quiet sadness entered her heart.

When her parents were taken from her, taken from this world, it was as if the whole world was eclipsed by that darkened shadow. She no longer wanted to run and jump into the land of the leaves. Her world had crashed down around her, leaving it pale gray like a sooty chimney in a crowded London of ancient times. This gray had filled her life, dulling it, making it less exciting, less happy, less alive.

Even though she was okay with her grandmother, who did the best she could, and had even managed to hang on to her love of music, she had always felt like her lifeblood had been slowed, darkened. It didn't run as quick, light, and fast as everyone else. She would look around and see carefree, spontaneous and happy people around her, while inside her, she always carried a certain percentage of melancholy that it seemed others did not. It was a darkness on the inside, which she was never sure how to eclipse. Was it even possible to return to the light? To revive it for someone who had been away and separate from it for so long?

Hannah leaned her bike against the outside brick wall of the library. It was a tall two-story building that almost looked like a Victorian house, with a stone-lined archway entrance and beautiful windows that reflected the sea. When she pulled open the door, a bell rang to announce her arrival.

"Welcome!" came a warm voice from among the book stacks. "Can I help you find anything today?" The woman's creamy skin and pleasant face were framed by tortoise-shell glasses and wisps of wavy brown hair that fell from a loose ponytail at the nape of her neck.

"I'm looking for Ashlin Aldona, the librarian?"

"Yes, I'm Ashlin," the woman said, smiling. Her eyes glowed with sincerity.

"Hi, I'm Hannah Skye, Jewelia's niece."

"I'm so sorry about your aunt being missing," Ashlin said as she placed a consoling hand on Hannah's shoulder. "How can I help you today?"

These well-intentioned words triggered a replay in Hannah's mind of all the times she'd been told people were sorry. Snapping out of it, she responded, "I'm looking to find out more about my family history, the island, and Halloween."

"Of course! We have a whole section dedicated to the town's history. Come check out aisle thirteen," Ashlin said as she walked across the room.

"Great, thanks." Hannah followed her, her fingers scanning the shelves.

Ashlin started grabbing books one by one. "Ah, here we are. *Exploring the Ancient Celtic Roots of Halloween: Samhain Revealed.*" She handed the book to Hannah, who scanned the introductory paragraphs:

> *Halloween originated from a pagan festival. The Celtic people of old revered this day as their New Year's Eve. It was in fact seen as the ending of the year. It was a time when the seasons shifted, summer's warmth waned, and the harvest came due, after which arrived the inevitable period of darkness and death that is part of the cycle of life. On Samhain, the Celts believed, the spirits of those who had passed on from this world would return to walk amongst us.*

This moment in time has often been described as a liminal doorway, a unique time stamp where the veil between the worlds is thinnest, allowing for an intermingling that is stronger and more potent than on any other day of the year. It was common practice to burn large bonfires as a sacred ritual offering to the deities, in hopes of ensuring the return of the sun and future abundance. The day was one on which the dead were honored and ac-knowledged.

Hannah looked up. "Wow, I've always known there was something special about Halloween!" She paged ahead.

The name Halloween is actually the result of attempts by other religious groups to squelch the traditions of the Celts. They created other holidays, moved them around on the calen-dar to be right next to pagan holidays, and attempted to replace the Celtic tradition with the observance of their own martyrs, whom they felt were more appropriate to honor. In an attempt to sway the Celts to follow suit, they called their new holiday All Saints' Day, placing it the day after Samhain, and borrow-ing the surrounding traditions from the Celts. But the true holiday still stood, undeterred by centuries of attempts to change it. Eventually Samhain took on a new name. Because All Saints' Day was The Feast of All Hallows, Samhain became All Hallows Eve, or Hallows

*Evening, and then ultimately was shortened to
the word Halloween.*

"Wow, I didn't know that!" Hannah exclaimed. She
was so glad to finally be researching this.

Ashlin was beaming at her, obviously eager to tell
her more. "The people here in Maple Hollow are direct
descendants of the Celtic lineage, so we have great reverence for Halloween," she began. "Our ancestors were
drawn to this island and believed it was a vortex, which
allowed them to access other realms and the Otherworld. When they settled here, they brought their
ancient traditions with them and charmed the island
to be a place of eternal autumn for those who dwell
here. The island has a continual harvest of pumpkins.
The trees lose all of their leaves by Halloween, but
then begin to sprout new ones starting November 1,
which grow in their natural colors of orange, red, and
yellow, year-round. No matter what attempts others
might have made to alter these beliefs and traditions,
we in Maple Hollow preserve our true origins and the
true history."

Hannah's eyes widened as she listened to Ashlin speak of the pumpkins. If there were pumpkins
year-round, that must have something to do with her
recurring dream.

"Maple Hollow is unique in this way, like no other
island or place in this earthly realm," Ashlin continued
with a secretive smile. "Because it has been dedicated
as such, we live in alignment with the spirits and there
is always reverence and acknowledgment of the physical death that must come to us all, all of us on this
earthly plane."

"Do you mean people come here to die, then?" Hannah asked, a bit confused by her mention of physical death.

Ashlin shook her head. "Death is a physical concept, an illusion created and promulgated by places outside of Maple Hollow. Those who dwell there may only receive a glimpse of what is possible one day a year, when they experience Halloween on the island. There is no spiritual death, which is why it is so important to acknowledge the spirits around us. Here in Maple Hollow, anything is possible at any time. Ancient cultures have celebrated this season and time for centuries and knew of its power, as well as its potential for tapping into the wisdom of the turning of the year. They also knew that the veil between the worlds, the seen and unseen, is thinnest on Halloween, that very special day of the year."

Then the librarian gently laid a pile of books down in front of Hannah and disappeared between the stacks.

Hannah sat in the library for hours, immersing herself in the books. It was as if time temporarily stopped. As anxious as she was to save her aunt, she knew she had to gain insight into the island's magick first, to be prepared for what she was up against.

She rode her bike away from the library as the sun dipped lower in the sky. She needed to ask Madame Morgan more questions. When she'd met her two days ago, Morgan had sparked something in her that she'd never experienced before. Hannah knew she was right; something was shifting in her, and fast. She still had so many questions.

She was also curious about Midnight. He had been following her around the manor since she arrived, as if he knew something. And then there was the talking cat she dreamed about, Wixby. She needed to ask Morgan about that. What was the significance of a piano-playing talking cat? She began to wonder if Morgan's cats talked, or if Midnight might talk.

As she approached the small metaphysical shop, the chimes blowing in the wind outside the door, she saw Milu sitting once again in the front window, watching the evening birds gather their twigs and branches. And as she entered the shop, Madame Morgan appeared right away. "Welcome back, Hannah," she said knowingly. "We have been waiting for you."

"We?" Hannah asked.

"Yes. My cats, Milu and Merlin, and I," she replied.

"Oh, right," Hannah quickly replied, not wanting to exclude the felines.

"Come sit, dear," Madame Morgan said, leading her back to the table they'd sat at before. A large pumpkin was in the middle, same as last time. "What questions have you brought me?" Morgan asked.

"Can cats talk?" Hannah blurted out, before she had time to plan a better way to ask it.

"Of course," Morgan replied.

"But I've never heard your cats talk." Hannah tried to keep her tone from sounding accusatory.

"Cats are special animals," Morgan began, waving her hands as she spoke. "Spirits, really, who communicate with us outside of our physical senses. Many people don't pay attention, but cats actually communicate with us energetically in a space that is beyond our body and physical mind. When we perceive them talking to us, it really is our mind translating their energetic messages into a physical language we can perceive with our physical mind. It's just our physical body helping us make sense of it, although they don't need our language at all, of course." Morgan explained.

"So...do you talk to Milu and Merlin?"

"Every day!" Morgan proclaimed, sweeping her scarf back around her neck.

"Can I talk to them?" Hanna asked.

"Maybe," Morgan replied. "It's a matter of attunement. Our spirit aligns us with certain animals for certain reasons, at certain times. If you are meant to and open to receiving their message, you will."

She smiled kindly. "There is something else as well." Hannah sensed that Morgan was about to offer something quite beyond anything she'd thought to ask. "In Maple Hollow, cats and pumpkins have a special connection. Because pumpkins are comparable in physical size to a cat's body, they can serve as a portal to transport the cats through space and time."

Hannah's ears perked up at the word "portal." "So, you mean cats can time travel?" she asked bluntly, attempting to unravel exactly what Morgan was explaining. "They can time travel through pumpkins?" she repeated more precisely.

"Yes, my dear. I see the truth is starting to reveal itself to you. This is a good sign of your transition," Morgan said reassuringly.

"So...do your cats time travel?"

"In fact they do!" Morgan laughed. "But we don't usually see it happen. Cats live in a netherworld that is between the worlds. It is their domain, which they traverse quite easily. It's called blinking. We can meet them on certain planes of existence, such as in dreams. To us it appears as if they are sleeping, but with the blink of an eye, they can actually travel through the Otherworld, beyond our comprehension of space and time. Cats have always had this ability, although most people don't want to acknowledge it."

"So how does it work?" Hannah pressed, even more curious now. She put her hand on the pumpkin.

"Cats must discover it for themselves. Sometimes they learn it by accident. The pumpkins in Maple Hollow are special. Unlike any other pumpkins in the entire world, they allow us to cross between worlds, and they also allow the cats of Maple Hollow to travel as well. This too will be revealed in time. The more you pay attention and open your mind, the more you will see," Madame Morgan concluded. With that, she stood up and disappeared into the back of the shop again.

Hannah sat for a moment staring at Milu and Merlin, watching their soft tails flop up and down, the breath of their bodies rise and fall, and their whiskers twitch as their extra senses buzzed with a hyper-awareness of their surroundings. They each, in their own time, blinked slowly. And Hannah blinked slowly back at them. She was discovering more, changing more, growing. She felt in her soul that what Madame Morgan had told her was true.

She rode back toward the manor. On the way, she noticed Detective Norma Nyx walking into a brick building. She decided to stop and investigate. There was just something off about Norma that she had to figure out. Leaning her bike under a nearby tree, Hannah snuck underneath an open window of the building. Norma was at a desk, her hair in a super-tight bun, not one hair out of place. She wore a drab and constricting suit, with no makeup or rings. But she did wear a silver necklace with a charm, and for a brief moment the setting sunlight caught on the charm. Hannah got a good look at the symbol on it, and she remembered seeing that symbol at the airport on someone's luggage.

In an instant, Hannah realized where she remembered Norma from. She was the woman in front of her in line at the check-in desk. Had Norma been following her? Had she followed her to Maple Hollow?

Norma's phone rang. Hannah listened as she answered it. "Yes, I'm here now in Maple Hollow," Norma said. "I'm on the case, sir. The girl arrived a few days ago and I've interviewed her. She doesn't know where her aunt is or about her lineage, and I'll make sure she doesn't find out."

Hannah could not make out what the voice on the other end of the line said in reply.

"Of course not, sir," Norma continued. "Quint Maytox and I will not fail in our mission. We will stop them once and for all." Then she promptly hung up the phone.

Hannah's heart began to pound in her chest at the words "we will stop them." Norma was not a detective. She was a Dream Haunter. So the Dream Haunters assumed human bodies to do their work? Norma and Quint Maytox were here in Maple Hollow for one reason and one reason only, to complete their mission and destroy the Skye family.

Hannah knew there was a reason she hadn't trusted the detective. Her intuition had been trying to tell her all along. And now she knew who was responsible for trapping Aunt Jewelia. As her aunt's letter had predicted, they were going to try to stop Hannah from rescuing Jewelia. They would make sure there was no way she could discover her aunt's whereabouts, or their evil intentions, or her family lineage, or most importantly, her power.

Jewelia's letter said her family had fought the Dream Haunters through the ages. The battle was as old as time. Her parents had to have known about it. Did they hide it from her to protect her? Probably. It was also probably why they didn't tell her much about Jewelia.

As Hannah rode home, the full moon rose in all its glory, filling nearly the whole horizon. It was so large and full, it truly looked like it was a planet about to collide with Earth. Her mind raced with everything she had discovered, and she struggled with what she must do next.

Chapter Fifteen

THE FOLLOWING FOG

Oct 25, 2007

It was nearing dusk, and Hannah had gone for a walk in the woods to clear her head after another day of poring over the library books. On her way there, she had stopped to watch the search boats that were still circling the island. While in the woods, she sat down on a fallen tree trunk to think. As she sat there looking about, the air began to thicken—first subtly, as if condensation was building up on her eyes like a film, then like a soft glow that seemed to gather in the air. It became thicker, forming around the tree trunks and between the leaves. The soothing sound of evening crickets hummed around her, and lightning bugs lit up the canopy of trees above her head.

As the fog started to surround her like a soft blanket, Hannah remembered Old Man Adams telling her on the ferry how important the fog was, that it allowed things unseen to be seen. And that when it rolled in, the veil it created that seemed to others to shroud, or hide, our world, in truth made other worlds more visible.

She ran her hands around in the fog and her fingertips touched leaves. She realized these were maple leaves. Of course they were—it was Maple Hollow, after all. There were hundreds if not thousands of maple trees all over the island. Hannah noticed that the bark below her was growing wet, and she decided she better head back.

As she neared the manor, the fog almost seemed to follow her. She felt a strong sense that perhaps there was something she was missing. Something she should be able to see, but had not. Something that could help her find Jewelia, if only it would reveal itself to her, or if only she knew where to look for the portal. She was not a cat—so did pumpkins hold that same magick for her? She needed to see what could not be seen. But how?

When Hannah entered the manor, she heard something that sounded like it was coming from the library. The walls echoed the whisper of a woman humming a soft tune. As she grew closer to the stairs, the sound faded more and more, until there was total silence when she touched the door to the library.

She entered the hallway, and the heavy door slammed behind her, giving her a start. A book dislodged from a bookshelf in the library and fell to the floor, landing open and face down. Hannah walked over and picked it up.

Magick, it read, *is the ritualized effort to align oneself with natural forces in the world in order to manifest an intention. It is the process through which one raises perceptions and ultimately finds the true destined path.* Hannah thought this made sense. But she realized it was a different explanation than she'd ever heard before. This magick wasn't the rabbit-out-of-the-hat type stuff she'd seen at carnivals. This was more spiritual, more personal, more authentic, like the magick of the island.

Perhaps Aunt Jewelia had been attempting to harness the storm, the energy of the sky, that night. Maybe she was trying to "manifest an intention" when she disappeared—her intention to stop the Dream Haunters.

Hannah walked to the other side of the library. She examined those books and grabbed one called *Spiritual Vortexes*. She flipped open the first page.

> *Spiritual vortexes are locations on the Earth filled with great spiritual energy. Normally appearing at the distinct intersection of meridians, they are known to produce spiritual awakening as well as grant access to the gates of the universe and other dimensions. Ancient civilizations knew the power of such places and honored locations such as the Pyramids of Egypt. Mystical and paranormal experiences are common near or inside vortex areas.*

This echoed what Ashlin had told her about her ancestors and the island. As she continued to walk around the library, Hannah noticed that she kept stepping on a particularly squeaky spot on the floor. It was near a globe perched on top of a gilded brass stand. The brass stand was burnished and shiny; the globe was embossed and lacquered. Hannah stepped closer to admire it and ran her fingers across the countries, seas and mountains. She thought about what it must be like to travel to, or even live in, such far-off places.

As she stepped back, she realized she was causing the floorboards to squeak again. This time she moved her foot back and forth. *Squeak squeak*, she heard. She knelt down and pressed her hand into the floor, seeing if she could replicate the noise. She pressed all her weight. *Squeak squeak*, she heard again.

She pulled back the Persian rug on the floor. It revealed a misshaped and discolored floorboard. It didn't match the others and was larger. She reached her nails into the grooves of the wood on the edges in an attempt to pry it up. Then she noticed, in the center, a handle folded down upon itself, so disguised as part of the wood grain that she hadn't even noticed it at first glance. It was a handle of a trap door.

Hannah grasped the handle and pulled. The panel opened toward her with a loud creak. Before her were stairs, leading down into inky blackness. Looking up, she spotted a lantern sitting on the mantle; it was within reach and there was a vase of long matches sitting next to it. Her aunt must have kept them there for when she too entered through this secret trap door. They were just like the match Midnight had brought her.

She struck the match, flames jumping with a spark, and inhaled the small puff of smoke as she lit the lantern. Holding it near her collarbone, she placed one foot on the first step below the trap door, then the other, then slowly descended as the darkness enveloped her shoulders.

Even with the light of the lantern, the stairway was dark and narrow. It spiraled in its descent and seemed to go on forever. Hannah carefully felt for each step, her heart pounding in her chest, her body surging with adrenaline in preparation for the unknown, what lay ahead, what lurked in the darkness, what she could not see. The further she descended, the colder it became. The air felt heavier, and dewy, a dank moisture making it thick.

Turning her head, she noticed illuminated by the light of the lantern were symbols carved into the walls along the stairway. She didn't recognize any of them, but she traced her fingers over some of them. The indentations seemed ancient, like they had been there thousands of years. But as she ran her fingers through them a feeling of connectedness came over her. Someone had carved these symbols, someone in the past, her past. A past she didn't know about yet, but that had always been there, waiting for her to discover it.

Finally, she reached the bottom of the stairs, the light glowing from the lantern in her right hand. To her surprise, in front of her now was a wall of books. It was as if whatever room lay behind this had been closed up and concealed. From ceiling to floor were shelves jam-packed with books, just like in the library upstairs. Hannah looked to her right, then her left, but saw only the stairwell walls. She pressed on the bookshelf built into the wall, but it did not give.

How could this be? she wondered. How could she get beyond this? Shouldn't this lead to a room or something? As Hannah stood silently, holding her lantern up in the darkness, the glow began to illuminate the book bindings. She scanned them quickly, her eyes moving over them like the lighthouse in the darkness of her dream.

She ran her fingers across the tops of the books, turning her head sideways to read the titles on the bindings:

*Unraveling the Secrets of Island Vortexes: An Insider's
Look*
Mirror Writing and the Art of Spellcasting
*From Time Travel to Alternate Realities: The Many
Forms of Interdimensional Travel*
Journeying Through Time and Space
And there was another one.

Deafening silence surrounded her. Hannah set the
lantern down on the hard floor, its handle clanking on
its cold metal, the circular orb of light now illuminating the dark floor. She reached with her right hand
for the book that had no title. It was larger than the
others and had Celtic knotwork down the spine. As
her fingers drew the top of the book spine toward her,
she heard a creaking noise that was not coming from
the stairs. It was coming from the shelf. She pulled it
further toward her, and as she did, the wall itself began
to give way, opening like a door.

It was a secret passageway. Hannah picked up the
lantern once more and stood in the doorway, staring
into the darkness. She had found a secret chamber in
the basement of her aunt's manor, and she was going
in.

Chapter Sixteen

THE SECRET ROOM

A s Hannah stepped inside, she realized she was in a small room. For such a large manor, she expected the basement to be very large, but this room was fairly small, like a workshop. The air was dank and still, the ground cold. There were no windows or lights. All the walls were just like the entrance she had come through, bookcases filled with books, from floor to ceiling. A small table stood to one side. The room really wasn't larger than an oversized closet. In the middle was a lectern, on top of which was a large book. Inscribed on the cover were the words *Grimoire de Skye*. On either side of the lectern stood two heavy marble statues in the shape of tall cats. They stood like guardians, regal and thin, like Egyptian goddesses watching over a treasure.

Hannah opened the book. The pages were brittle and worn, as if the book was centuries old. She flipped through the pages, not exactly sure what she was looking for. The book, which seemingly had a life of its own, had flopped open to a page near the middle. It was as if this part had been accessed more than the rest, the spine of the book opening naturally to this section.

There were pictures of pumpkins, and diagrams, next to which it said *Tairseach an Phuimcín*. It appeared to be instructions on how to carve a pumpkin, in a language she didn't know. But Hannah knew it couldn't be as simple as that. Why was there a book in a basement room with her family name on it about making jack-o'-lanterns? The title made it sound like much more.

She closed the book and slung it under her arm, grabbed her lantern, and walked back toward the stairs. As she approached the staircase, the bookshelf door began to close behind her, as if it had a wisdom of its own and knew she was leaving. By the time she had both feet on the steps, it had fully closed, removing any trace of the hidden room. It once again looked like a bookshelf, granted in quite an unusual place.

Hannah climbed the stairs, faster now, clutching the book to her chest, rising out of the darkness.

CHAPTER SEVENTEEN

THE BOOK

OCTOBER 26, 2007

The next morning, Hannah rode into town, the book inside the basket attached to the bicycle. She would be sure to safely return it later to the secret room. Maybe Ashlin knew what it all meant. As she entered the library, the bell on the door rang, and Ashlin popped up from behind the counter to greet her.

"Well, hello again, Hannah. What can I help you with today, on this full Hunter's Moon?"

Hannah pushed the book across the counter toward Ashlin. "I found this in a secret room in the manor, but I can't read it. Do you know what it means?" She flipped to the section it had opened to before.

Ashlin adjusted her glasses and placed her hands on the book. "Wow, this is a very old book indeed. Let's see. For starters, *Grimoire de Skye*, that's Irish for Grimoire of Skye. A grimoire is traditionally a book of magickal instructions that is passed down within a family."

"And this? Are these instructions on how to make a jack-o-lantern?" Hannah pointed to the pumpkin diagrams.

"*Tairseach an Phuimcín* is also Irish, and literally means Portal of the Pumpkin. Have you considered the sacred nature of the Halloween celebration? As you know, Maple Hollow was created as a sanctuary to protect ancient Celtic traditions. But more than that, the families that founded it were also protecting their own legacies. Each with its own legends and magick. If you can decipher what the book is trying to teach you..." Ashlin paused thoughtfully. "If you can decipher it, you may be one step closer to discovering what happened to your aunt."

***

Aunt Jewelia followed the old ways. She had been taught by her grandmother when she was just a girl. Her parents had passed when she was young, then later her brother and his wife. Jewelia resolved as a young woman that she wouldn't allow this tragedy to keep happening. She also believed that the best way, and in fact the only way, to make sure the cycle did not repeat was to not involve any other family members. She was going to end the attacks on her family herself. She would fight and defeat the Dream Haunters once and for all. If she succeeded, or if she failed, no one else needed to know. No one else needed to suffer and no one else needed to die at the hands of the Dream Haunters.

This was, in part, why she never sought out her niece Hannah. She also respected her brother's wishes to protect his family from danger. Jewelia figured it was better, safer, if she took on the malevolent forces herself. She would shoulder the burden; then no one else had to. She would protect her family through her own sheer will and skill, through her own mind and body. Then the threat would be no more.

Jewelia felt the Dream Haunters had no right to interfere with people's dreams and lives. Why should they know everyone's fears and wishes, insecurities and challenges? She knew dreams had their own power, but it was a power that was meant for the dreamer, not the business of a nefarious outside ruler. Yet she couldn't fully protect dreamers on her own. The onus was ultimately on each dreamer, and it was her family's unique legacy to empower others to grow through their dreams. They were Healers who showed people the way. Once people had free reign in their dreams and could dream as much as they wanted, they could take the next step to evolve. If they paid attention to their dreams, listened to the meanings, and translated the dreams to help with decisions in their waking life, the Dream Haunters would lose their power. They would no longer be able to control dreams, track them, or trap people within them. If each dreamer stopped discarding their dreams, stopped dismissing them as pedantic, pointless, and imaginary, they would then be embracing their own power, their own agency, their own ownership, their own life path.

Dreams were never meant to be fodder for the Dream Haunters. They were meant for each dreamer, and that dreamer alone. But over time, as centuries passed, people had stopped listening to their dreams, stopped giving them credence, stopped valuing them; in fact, they stopped to the point that they actually convinced themselves they didn't dream at all. This was exactly what the Dream Haunters wanted. Once the ownership was relinquished, the importance of dreams diminished, the Dream Haunters were free to roam and reign as they saw fit. They could track and observe dreams, pick the one dream that was the most perplexing, most disturbing, most depressing, most deflating, and it was that dream they would choose to trap the dreamer in. Trap them so they could never escape and start to believe the dream was the truth. And they could do this even while the dreamer was awake, causing them to vanish, as if they were sucked into another dimension, their physical body vaporized from physical existence.

The dreamer then no longer would have a waking life. Only an existence inside that dream, that nightmare. That is where they would dwell for the rest of their days. This was the goal of the Dream Haunters' dark energy. Dream deniers unknowingly opened the door to them and welcomed them in.

That night under the full moon, Hannah fell asleep flipping through her family's grimoire. She found herself on a dark street. It was a downtown area, but not where she lived, nor Maple Hollow. The buildings were taller. Towering, in fact, in a much bigger city. All the first floors of the buildings were a reddish-brown type of brick on the outside. The taller skyscrapers were metal and had tons of lights, like a skyline at night. Blue lines wrapped around the buildings at different heights and tiny white or gold windows were illuminated throughout.

As she walked the street, she was trying to get back to her apartment, but for some reason she couldn't remember the way and had become disoriented. Initially she started walking straight, thinking that was the way. But then as she looked further down the street she realized she didn't recognize anything and thought it couldn't be the right way. She assured herself she'd just taken a wrong turn, turned around, and headed the other way.

But as she went the other way down the street, again she felt she didn't recognize anything. That wasn't right either.

She looked down a side street. Had she perhaps taken a turn somewhere to get to this street and she needed to backtrack? Down the side street she saw a man in the glow of the street light. When he saw her, he retreated into the darkness.

I better not go down there, she thought to herself. *He'll be waiting if I do, waiting in the darkness.*

So instead, she decided to cut through a sushi restaurant. It was the only thing that appeared open and she thought it would be safer than being out on the street. As she walked into the restaurant, two people stood at a lectern, their heads jerking up as she entered. She wasn't intending to stay, so she turned past them and walked into the restaurant. But when she couldn't find her way through, she decided to head back out to the street. There was an intense smell of strange exotic fish. As she walked down an exit corridor, she noticed she was barefoot. Her feet were soggy and wet, slimy in fact, as if she had been walking on the ocean's bottom.

CHAPTER EIGHTEEN

THE CABIN

OCTOBER 27, 2007

When Hannah awoke, she reached for her phone to text Maggie. "Hey, are you awake?" "Yeah, how's it going?" Maggie quickly replied.

"I've been researching and finding a ton of interesting books. Have you ever heard of Mercury retrograde?" Hannah asked.

"I think so, I had a friend that was really into astrology in college and she would always tell me when it was that time. She seemed to think it had the power to affect things in her life, but I'm not sure about that," Maggie responded.

"It can be intense. When I was flying here my flight was delayed, but I didn't think anything of it," Hannah said. "But there's more."

"Do tell," Maggie implored.

"I found a secret room in the manor, under the library," Hannah typed slowly. "There's definitely something going on here, but I can't say more until I'm sure."

"A secret room! How cool is that?!" Maggie exclaimed. "You always seem to find a new mystery. Be careful, okay?"

"Always," Hannah typed, setting her phone down and looking out the window.

***

As the day wore on, Hannah grew more desperate. She needed to do something, but didn't know what. Out the bedroom window she could see the large maple trees. It was the kind of day when the sun shined brightly but the air was cold to the lungs. A light breeze wafted through the trees surrounding the manor, which were glowing with the warm shades of autumn: gold, red, spots of brown, and flecks of purple. The sea beyond the trees glistened, unaffected by the changing temperature, sun or shadow.

Hannah set out in the late hours of the afternoon on a slow walk toward town. She had more questions for Ashlin. But when she arrived, there was a sign on the door that said *Sorry library closed due to illness.* "Of course it's closed," she said under her breath, frustrated that she was stalled yet again. In a huff, she turned away and began to head back toward the manor.

The sun was setting earlier now that Halloween was getting closer. Long shadows cast themselves across the side streets as she walked along the main drag. The quaint lantern lights lining the sidewalks were flickering on. As she walked, Hannah started to sense that something wasn't right. She kept looking behind her, feeling as if she was being watched. Seeing things in her periphery, just out of sight, she began to quicken her pace. She kept seeing the shadows of what appeared to be various men standing along the sidewalk, but when she'd look back, there wasn't anyone there. Their stature was ominous and threatening, and an uncomfortable feeling spread inside her. She had the strange feeling they were watching her, following her. She decided to take a detour into the woods to get out of sight.

Yet once she got off the sidewalk, she could definitely hear footsteps behind her. She began to decipher, within the crunching of the leaves, which steps were her steps and which were caused by other hastening feet. Instinctively, she jumped behind a large maple tree. Looking back, her eyes caught the shadow of someone behind her.

Hannah's breath quickened and her heart started to pound. She recognized in an instant the reality of the situation: she *was* being followed. Now she had to run, she had to run for it and get away before whoever it was caught up to her, whatever they were planning on doing.

She bolted. Running now as fast as she could, swerving between the trees, nearly running into some at times, using her arms to break small branches in her way, the jagged edges scraping the flesh of her forearms as she ran. Her ankles wobbled as she stepped into small holes and uneven ground on the forest floor. The faster she ran, the faster was the swishing behind her of someone in pursuit, apparently increasing their speed to keep up. She didn't have time to look back; she couldn't look behind her for fear they'd be breathing down her neck. She thought that if she could just get out of the woods, to an opening, the clearing and the manor grounds, whoever was following her might not risk being exposed.

Then, through the trees, she saw the lights of the manor. She ran even faster as the evening began to envelope the forest, the corners of it folding up like a dark abyss around her as the daylight quickly receded. She finally stepped out of the forest onto the dewy green carpet of grass on the manor grounds. She was still in the shadows, but out of the woods.

She could see Old Man Adams' cabin nearby, the light glowing from the windows. Her breath was now frosting the air as she ran the final distance toward it.

Then Hannah saw there was an even closer escape than the cabin. A small shed stood in her path. She would hide there. She bolted toward the shack. It was shrouded in fog, its shingles cracked and worn from the island weather. She could see the dark depths of the doorway, waiting open for her to escape.

As she crossed the threshold, she was immersed in total darkness. She felt like she had plunged into a deep sea, inky blackness all around her. Her hands fumbled as she felt around in the dark. Reaching in front of her, she silently placed a wish that she would not kick or knock anything over and accidentally draw attention to her hiding spot. Quietly, she attempted to feel what she couldn't see. Remembering how her grandmother had shown her to walk on the ice when she was child, she intently avoided sliding her feet along the floor and instead took short choppy steps, raising her feet in the air before placing them down, adopting a nearly military-type march.

There was a small window on the wall next to the door. Hannah crouched down next to it and peered outside. She stared into the woods in the distance, waiting, her heart thumping in her chest. Then she saw it: movement in the woods. She could hardly make it out through the grimy thin window of the shack, but she could see the shadow of a figure. It became clearer the closer it came. Then she could see a defined outline of a person, at first running, then slowing to a walking pace. They were large in stature, tall, from their silhouette. But she could not see a face or anything identifying. Then for some reason, as they approached the clearing, they turned abruptly and headed back, disappearing into the darkness.

Hannah knew this was her chance to get to safety. She exited through the dark doorway and began to run toward Old Man Adams' cabin. She could see a soft white plume of smoke rising from the chimney, and the lights inside seemed so warm and inviting compared to the danger she felt outside. She could see her own breath in the moonlight as she ran as fast as her legs would take her. When she got to the burly wood cabin door, she knocked rapidly and loudly with her bare knuckles.

Old Man Adams opened the door, a look of shock on his face. "Hannah? Come in, come in." He extended his hand to guide her in and quickly grabbed a blanket from an armchair nearby, wrapping it around her shoulders. "What happened?" he asked, looking searchingly into her eyes.

"Someone's chasing me," Hannah uttered, her heart and lungs still so tight in her chest that they resisted expanding to let any more air in. "But they ran away when I made it to the shed."

"No one should be out there, Hannah. But I'm happy to check."

Adams slowly walked toward the window, pulling back the curtains now to peer into the darkness. He opened the front door and grabbed a large flashlight from a table next to it, then passed back and forth a bit on the front deck, flashing his light to and fro.

Hannah's hands trembled, adrenaline circulating despite her best efforts to squelch it. As she waited for Adams to come inside and close the door, all she could think about was the Dream Haunters.

When Adams crossed the threshold Hannah continued to explain, "I couldn't see who it was…but they followed me home from town. I went to the library to try to find out more about my family, but it was closed," she said, looking down in frustration. But then she looked up at Old Man Adams, and saw, across the room, a hutch filled with nearly hundreds of picture frames.

"Perhaps *you* could help me," she said, marveling at all of the photos. She stood up, crossed the room, and grabbed one of the frames in her still slightly shaking hands.

"Any way that I can," Old Man Adams replied, his tone more solemn now but gentle.

"Who are all these people?" Hannah asked.

"Well, my dear," he began, taking a deep breath, "I've been here a long time." He seemed as if he was about to embark on an epic journey of a saga too winding to relate in a short format. "While I'm not directly related to your family, I do consider them my family in a nostalgic sort of way, since I don't have one of my own. Over the years I've grown close to your aunt and almost see her as the daughter I never had." As he spoke, a wrinkle of sadness, grief, and regret passed over his brow and eyes, landing on his lips in a sorrowful frown.

"I guess I feel responsible about that night. I should have stopped her."

"Who is this in the picture?" Hannah asked as she picked up another frame. It had two young men sitting side by side, one's arm around the other, both in army clothing. The faded orange and brown of the photo made the setting hard to decipher, but Hannah could tell they were in wartime.

"That's me and your grandfather, Jewelia's father Witt. We fought together in the war." Adams slowly walked over to join Hannah near the hutch.

"My grandfather?" Hannah blurted. She'd known her grandmother on her mother's side, but she hadn't known either of her grandfathers. She may have seen pictures long ago, but at this moment she didn't recognize him.

"When we fought in the war together, I made a promise to Witt, as brothers, that I would always look after his children, that being Jewelia and your father. I have tried with all my might to keep that promise. When Witt and his wife passed suddenly, I came here to the manor to live with Jewelia, so she wouldn't be all alone. But I failed with your father, and now I've failed your aunt. I have such guilt about something happening to her. I can't break that promise to him. He always looked out for me, would give his life for my safety. I owe him as much," Adams said, wringing his hands. A look of woe and worry came over his face again.

Hannah felt his sadness. It was easy for her to take on other people's emotions, in a way that maybe not everyone did. She used to think it was the same for everyone, but the older she got the more she realized it wasn't. There was something called sympathy or compassion, but that wasn't quite it. She actually embodied other people's emotions, like a transfer of energy into her body. She took it on like a heavy albatross on her shoulders. She carried it like the heavy backpack in her dream. Someone else's luggage was always added on. She was the spiritual porter for others. She couldn't help but put her hand on Old Man Adams' shoulder.

"You will keep your promise," she said, almost surprising herself. "I'm going to find out what happened to her, and we will find her."

Adams looked up at her. "Thank you, little lady, I do hope so," he said, clapping his hand over hers in the assuring way older people tended to do. "And we need to find out who was following you. My promise to protect Witt's children extends to you." He squeezed her hand.

Hannah stared into Old Man Adams' eyes and saw something she hadn't seen in years. In her soul she felt it to be true—he *would* protect her, and his calling to watch over the manor and Aunt Jewelia was his struggle. He'd never had children of his own; her father and Aunt Jewelia were his children now; and she was by this principle his granddaughter. As she soaked in the comfort of the cabin and the warmth of his weathered hand on hers, a feeling of security swept over Hannah and she knew, now more than ever, that she was where she was supposed to be.

"Why don't you stay here tonight," he offered. "Make yourself at home," he said, showing her to a bedroom down the small hallway.

Hannah, exhausted from the scare, finally went to bed and fell asleep.

H annah was standing in the manor, looking out a large window. It was slightly cracked open, letting the sweet night air waft in. The glowing white moon rose high, speckled with dark craters, casting a foggy glow through the opening. Below that she saw a mountain backdrop that was darkened against a purple sky. Off in the distance were white peaks, then dark hatches of trees scattered up the inclines. Tiny stars twinkled against the gradient navy-blue sky overhead, blending to a light violet as it merged with the horizon.

As she stood at the window, she noticed on the sill a single candle on a wrought-iron holder. Its flame mesmerized her as it wafted on the ever-so-gentle breeze. Also on the sill was a collection of crystals, neatly placed, some white like the moon, some a light turquoise blue like the ocean on a bright day. Translucent white curtains hung over the window on either side and gently undulated in the evening breeze. A wind chime gently tousled, giving off a sweet song.

Through the window, she could see what looked like a magickal garden: bushes, flowers, and plants of all shapes and sizes. What looked like tiny white moths or butterflies scurried around the plants, gathering up their evening pollen. Evening flowers began to open their eyes to the setting sun, blossoming amid the darkness. The gentle hum of crickets vibrated in the distance. She felt peaceful dwelling in this place.

But suddenly the moon was so large it seemed like she was on another planet. It was rising up from the horizon ahead of her, and she realized she was no longer standing in the manor; instead, there was now water all around her. It was as if she was in a boat, but she could see nothing holding her, just the waves undulating and crashing toward her.

CHAPTER NINETEEN

THE FREQUENCIES

OCT 28, 2007

When Hannah awoke, she immediately thought of Madame Morgan. She must go back and see her again. She had to ask about her aunt, about the people—if they were people—that were chasing her, and about the manor.

Old Man Adams must have been out on the grounds, as she didn't see him anywhere. She walked back to the manor, grabbed some fruit from the kitchen, and rode her bike quickly toward town. The morning air was chilly but felt fresh and clean. The rising sun was low in the sky still, dashing a bright pastel painting on the horizon. She realized she wasn't even sure if Madame Morgan's shop was open yet, plus it was a Sunday. But when she arrived, she saw her standing in the doorway with a knowing look.

"Greetings, Hannah," Morgan said, beckoning her in. Merlin paced around Morgan's ankles as she turned and headed inside.

"Oh, Madame Morgan...I'm so glad you're here. I really need to know more about Aunt Jewelia."

"I know, my dear. I sensed you would be coming back, and this morning. I knew it was time."

"How did you know I was coming?"

"The universe guides us at all times, my dear. All we need to do is listen," Morgan replied with a comforting wink. "Come in now and have a seat. I have something to show you."

She walked to the table, Merlin prancing ahead as if he was excited about the revelation to come. She pulled out the upholstered velvet chair. "It is time," she said again.

"Time for what?" Hannah asked cautiously. Having been chased through the woods the night before, she wasn't sure she was ready for any other challenges at this point. She *was* sure there was something she innately knew, but was somehow separated from it. It was like there were tiny puzzle pieces missing, or she was missing the map to the puzzle. Was she separating herself or was the world standing in her way?

"Time for you to discover your power. Your ancestral lineage and path." Madame Morgan sat down on the adjacent chair, Merlin jumping immediately into her lap. On the table was the pumpkin. It had a perfect round shape, a vibrant orange color, and a perfect large stem.

"Milu would like to come sit on your lap, if you'll oblige," Morgan added, diverting her eyes toward the floor where the cat sat, looking up at Hannah and waiting for approval.

"Of course." Hannah patted her lap. Milu jumped up and curled into a tight ball, making himself immediately comfortable.

"The animals of Maple Hollow are part of a long line dating back to the founding families of the island,"

Morgan said with a smile. "They serve as our guardians or familiars, guides to the other realms. Milu knows of your power. That's why he brought you the pumpkin toy last time you were here. I'd like you to place your hands on the pumpkin now," she continued, now speaking in a slow, meditative voice. "Close your eyes and take some deep breaths with me. Relax your mind. Begin to focus on your mind's eye, your third eye. Go inward, my dear. You must go deep."

Moments passed. The patient hands of an antique clock nearby slowly ticked along in the silence. The faint glisten of chimes blowing in the gentle morning breeze echoed from outside the building. Hannah sat as still and as quiet as she could, her hands gently cradling the pumpkin on either side.

"Now I want you to clear your mind. It is time for you to align yourself with the frequencies of the island. It is a vortex. It is very powerful. You must now harness the connection. Use the pumpkin as your portal. It is your conduit to the other worlds unseen. Use your breath to keep your mind clear, until you can no longer. Then tell me what the first image is that you see."

There was a long pause. Hannah sat quietly, trying not to focus on the words Madame Morgan had spoken. Aunt Jewelia had said in her letter to open a portal, and now this was all she could think about.

"I see a dark place," she replied eventually. "It's almost like a prison cell, but it's very old. The walls are stone. There is no light. I can't see anything."

"Good, Hannah. Now tell me what you feel right now. What do you sense in your heart?" Madame Morgan asked.

"I feel a great sadness. It's almost like hopelessness, filled with fear, shame, and doubt. It's overwhelming and seems to be dripping from the walls," Hannah said softly.

"Now, Hannah, I am going to raise your vibration. Keep your hands on the pumpkin and follow your breath. Continue to breathe deeply. It will align your spirit with your body," Madame Morgan instructed.

Hannah took a deep breath. As she did, she began to fill a familiar tingle that started at her feet. They felt cool, as if she had just stepped barefoot into a cold spring. The tingle rose past her knees, up her legs to her hips, and then her whole spine began to tingle. It was electric. She wanted to open her eyes but resisted the temptation. She didn't want to break the connection.

"Hannah, I need you now to open your heart. Think of something that makes you happy, someone you love, a place that makes you feel safe and comforted, or a moment in time where you felt grateful and secure."

Hannah thought of her childhood cat Mystera. She felt the weight of her eyelids become heavier as her body began to feel lighter. She didn't even have to try at this; it was just happening for her. Her heart began to fill with warmth. It was as if someone was blowing a heater from inside her body, or as if she had stepped up to a radiant hearth, the heat emanating into her chest. A fantastic combination of warmth and chills enveloped her body. It was like nothing she had ever felt before. It was magickal, mystical, ethereal.

"You are surrounded now by spirits. They are your spirit guides, here to help you," Morgan quietly told her. "You are a guide, a healer. You have always had this ability, as it is part of your heritage. It is only revealing itself now. The pumpkin is your portal. It is your doorway to other dimensions. You are very special and very, very gifted. Now is the time for you to claim your power. To step through this portal of interdimensional mystery and walk the other worlds. It is your duty as a Healer of the Hollow. You must save those trapped in their dreams."

Suddenly there was a large slam. The front door slammed shut and the candles that had been lit blew out, leaving them shrouded in darkness. Hannah opened her eyes and looked at Madame Morgan in alarm.

"Do not be alarmed, my dear, you have done well. You can now remove your hands from the pumpkin."

Hannah slowly released her grip, and Milu jumped off her lap. Then she noticed that the pumpkin appeared to have almost been carved—an image of a castle was etched on its surface in the rind, revealing the moist flesh underneath. "How did that happen?" Hannah exclaimed.

"It is called a *cló aisling*, or "dream print" in Irish. It's a symbolic representation of the world you entered. It leaves an impression, a sort of metaphysical mark upon the pumpkin. The sorrowful place you just traveled to was a dream. Not your own dream, but someone else's. They were trapped there. The feelings you felt were theirs. You energetically received their emotions and were able to tap into their dimensional location. By opening your heart, you released them from their trap. This is evident by the emblem now carved into the pumpkin. The *cló aisling* is the remnant, what is left when the dreamer is released. They are free now, Hannah. You have done your part."

Hannah's eyes widened as she stared at Madame Morgan in shock. "So jack-o'-lanterns really aren't just carved for fun," she said.

"That is what happens in modern times, but the ancient origins of the practice lie with our people. This is how it has been done for centuries. You, Hannah, are a Healer of the Hollow," Madame Morgan repeated.

"But what does that mean? What am I supposed to do? Is this how I can find and save Aunt Jewelia?" Hannah began to feel stress rising up and her chest tightened.

"Patience, my dear. You do not have to force this. It will be easier if you allow it to flow through you, like a river. Soon it will be second nature. For now, go back to the manor and rest. Everything will happen in time as it is supposed to." Madame Morgan rose from the chair. Merlin wound around her ankles. She disappeared once more behind the curtain.

Hannah sat in silence. The ticking of the clock and the ringing of the chimes began to blend together into a harmonious sync. Tears rose in her eyes as she allowed the energetic emotions to flow through her.

Madame Morgan is right, she thought. *This is what I have always known. This is why I came here. This is how I will save Aunt Jewelia.*

***

Back at the manor, so many thoughts raced through Hannah's mind. She felt electric with excitement, anticipation, and anxiety all at the same time. She thought about how she felt when she first arrived. The tingling sensation when she had first touched her feet to the ground when stepping off the boat with Old Man Adams. Images of the twisted, gnarled trees they had driven by now flashed through her mind. She was beginning to understand what a vortex was; it made perfect sense.

Madame Morgan's words echoed in her mind: *Align yourself with the frequencies of the island.* The words *harness the connection* repeated on a loop in Hannah's mind. She could hear the words in her inner ear, and she felt uncertainty and fear that she wouldn't be capable of doing whatever it was Madame Morgan expected her to be able to do. The more minutes that passed, the more doubts began to creep in. Had she gone through the portal on her own? Or had Madame Morgan made it happen? If she had done it herself, how?

Then a warm blanket of solace enveloped her. She thought back to Madame Morgan's directive to *discover your power.* She always knew there was something more to her than what everyone else thought, that she was different, not completely of this world but partly in the next, or Otherworld. She could see things, feel things, sense things, that others could not. She had the innate ability to question, to seek, to ask of the unknown more than others would dare. She had been led here to discover all of this, at this exact time in her life, in this exact place, because it was her ultimate test. She didn't have a choice in the matter; she was being called, and now she had to answer.

Hannah ducked under the stairs to the library door, Midnight following as she entered. Once inside, she slid her fingers across the ancient spines of the books, scanning the titles, looking for anything about sound. She remembered seeing something the last time she was there, but she had no idea where, and there were books literally to the ceiling as well as stacked all around her on the floor.

A creeping feeling of frustration and anxiety began to take hold in her neck. As she strained to read the titles above her line of sight, she grasped the back of her straining neck. Midnight jumped up onto the desk, watching and waiting.

Hannah stood in front of the stacks of books, waiting for direction.

It was then that she noticed the thumping of Midnight's tail. His eyes serene as a still pond, he stared straight through Hannah, waiting for her to step outside her turbulence and notice what was right in front of her. She looked at Midnight. The sound of his tail on the books was louder now.

"Midnight," she exclaimed, reaching out to pat him on the head. "Thank you, that is just what I was looking for."

His tail was thumping on the spine of a book entitled *Vibration Frequencies: Aligning for Activation.*

She grabbed the book with both hands and settled into an opulent armchair. The fall wind howled outside, the leaves occasionally blowing against the window like a bat in the night. But Hannah was never distracted; she was intrigued by the wisdom. It consumed her. As a pianist, she knew quite a bit about sound waves and music, but she had never stopped to consider what the actual effect of it might be on our mind, body, and spirit, much less our existence.

She read about an ancient set of sound frequencies that were used for healing and transformation, each one holding its own power: *Frequencies are often measured in hertz, or the number of cycles per second within a sound's waveform,* she read. Always fascinated with the unseen, she felt almost validated to learn that certain sound waves as well as light waves were not visible or audible to humans. The pages also revealed the secrets of the power of certain frequencies, such as 432 Hz, sometimes called the frequency of the universe, and its ability to align our DNA with earthly energies, unlock our intuition, and access spiritual wisdom. That must be what Madame Morgan was talking about. It all started to make sense. Perhaps musical notes were more powerful than she had ever considered.

She spent hours studying the different frequencies and their uses. She thought back to the music from her recent dreams, both the piano music in her lantern dream and Wixby playing the piano. Could it be possible that Jewelia had knowledge of the dimensional powers of musical notes? Maybe she could harness them to save her. All these thoughts swirled in Hannah's mind as she continued to soak up the words from the pages.

She thought about her experience with Madame Morgan. She felt empowered and yet still filled with uncertainty. It was like someone had given her a map to a treasure, assuming she would be able to find her way, but she didn't know where the path began and where the road was for her to start on.

She tried to concentrate on the image that had arisen, of the prison cell, and all the ways she had experienced it with her senses. Then she heard Madame Morgan's words echo in her head: *Patience, my dear. You do not have to force this.* So maybe even this counted as trying too hard. She was so used to making things happen through struggle and effort, it was strange now to have someone say it would just happen, and in fact possibly happen easier through not trying.

Images of the sea surrounding the manor grounds rose in Hannah's mind's eye. She thought back to the dream she had the night before, of the moon out the window. The dream had gone from being at the manor and feeling peaceful to feeling helpless at sea.

It will be easier if you allow it to flow through you, like a river.

Taking Morgan's advice, Hannah imagined releasing her body to the sea and floating on top of the ebb and flow of the water. This helped relax her body and began to fill her with a sense of calm.

Soon, it will be second nature. For now, go back to the manor and rest. Everything will happen in time as it is supposed to, Madame Morgan had said.

She's right, I must rest now, Hannah thought. It was the only way she would be able to help Aunt Jewelia.

She drifted off to sleep in the chair and had a most unusual dream.

The sun was high in the sky and the clouds slowly marched across the horizon like a parade, each minute forming new shapes: one minute a white rabbit and the next minute a castle of ice. Hannah sat in the weeds. She noticed, peeking out over a large rock, what appeared to be a tiny lizard head. She watched it bob its head up and down, catching flies for a snack, and walked closer to get a better look. The lizard wasn't a lizard at all. It was a tiny turtle. She had only been able to see his head.

"Good day," she heard a voice say in what sounded like a British accent.

"Good day," Hannah said, spinning around, expecting to find the one delivering the greeting standing behind her. However, there was no shadow, no person, and no one around.

"Good day," she heard again, with a bit of a stammer. This was followed by an incessant tapping. It was the turtle! To Hannah's surprise, the turtle was smacking his tiny tail in frustration attempting to assert himself.

"Well, hello," Hannah said. "My name is Hannah, nice to meet you."

"And I, Abernathy," the tiny turtle replied with all the courtesy of a royal page. "Pleasure to make your acquaintance." Then he jumped into the pond and went for a swim.

Hannah stared at the bright green, richly hued grass. The sun was illuminating a bright stripe, almost like a walkway. It seemed more alive than the rest. As her gaze followed the path, her eye was drawn to the edge of the pond. Yet the glow didn't stop there. It continued into the water. The reflection glistened with the dancing light. Then she saw it—something in the pond brighter than the fertile grass. Something was catching the light as the wind softly blew the shifting sands.

"It's beautiful, isn't it?" Abernathy said as he returned to shore.

"What is it?" Hannah asked.

"I can oblige you with a closer look."

Hannah nodded excitedly. Abernathy stood up from his perch on a smooth pink rock that had gotten rather warm from the sun. He dove into the water again. Seemingly effortlessly, he glided down to where the shiny item lay waiting. When he emerged from the water, Hannah could see he was carrying something in his mouth. He dropped it on the warm rock.

It was an old skeleton key. She grasped it, admiring the ornate design and engraving. "This is beautiful," she said.

"Consider it a gift." Abernathy bowed the best a turtle could.

"Why thank you, Abernathy, it's lovely." She tucked it into her pocket.

Chapter Twenty

THE DIMENSIONS

Oct 29, 2007

W hen Hannah awoke in the library, it was still dark. She grabbed some nearby loose paper. She had kept a dream journal since she was quite young and always recorded her dreams. She loved writing down her thoughts, good or bad, in general; it always had a way of soothing her.

She wrote of Abernathy, the tiny turtle she had met in her dream. She remembered how distinguished he was, so wise for being so small. She wrote of the key he had gifted her. Aunt Jewelia's letter echoed in her mind: *discover the key.*

Madame Morgan had unlocked something inside her. An innate ability that was uniquely hers. It was meant to be. She now believed Morgan's words: *You are a guide, a healer.* Now she knew it was part of her heritage. That she hadn't gained this ability, she had simply remembered it. She had been led to the island to align with its vortex energy, and it was all perfectly synced the way it was supposed to be.

Her dream about the pumpkin patch was a premonition of her ancestral power, and also her duty to wield that power. It was her gift.

Now is the time for you to claim your power.

It wasn't just her aunt that she was here to save; it was so much bigger than that. And it was definitely more than an interesting diversion from finding a so-called "job." It was for a higher purpose. Her higher purpose.

Hannah now had to embrace her duty as a Healer of the Hollow, to step through the "portal of interdimensional mystery" and walk the other worlds. There were millions of people who needed her help, who were waiting for her to finally wake up to why she was here. She must now save those trapped in their dreams. She must now open the portal and save Aunt Jewelia.

But it was dark still, and her mind and eyes were heavy. She went upstairs to rest for a while longer in her bed, thoughts spiraling around in her head. In her dream, Abernathy had given her a silver key. Was this the key Aunt Jewelia was referring to?

She began to drift back toward sleep, but it wasn't really sleeping at all.

As Hannah floated within the dimensional space between waking and sleeping, she began to see a scene in her mind. She felt the presence of someone else. In her mind's eye, she saw a dark room. It was more like a prison, cold, dark, and gray. Her bones chilled and her breath filled the air like a cloud of fog.

The sound of clinking metal drew her attention and she turned to see a young woman sitting in a dark corner of the room, on the floor, her head down.

Throughout her whole body, Hannah felt a very strong urge to help.

She looked down at her hands. It was something she did often, a technique she had read about in a book a long time ago, a way to confirm, or in this case de-confirm, the existence of reality. When she did, she saw that in her left hand she was grasping a key. It was the key Abernathy gifted her in her dream. Except this time, she could make out three letters engraved on the key.

AGB

Her first thought was that they must be someone's initials, a shorthand clue for a much longer name. But who? As she stared at the key, the scene around her began to shift.

She now stood in front of an ancient-looking bookshelf. What made this bookshelf different was that it had glass panels protecting each level. Upon closer inspection she saw that each level was locked. A flash of inspiration came over Hannah and she inserted the key into the first lock. To her surprise, the glass door opened, slowly sliding out of place to reveal the row of books, which were even more ancient-looking than the shelf itself. She stared at them in wonder.

Hannah awoke once more and turned over in bed. It seemed like she had been lying there for hours, tossing about as thoughts ran through her head.

Nearly an hour later, as she drifted off to sleep, she entered yet another dream.

T his time she heard the faint sound of music. At first, she thought it might have been the radio of an alarm clock, but there was no such thing in her guest room at the manor. She realized it was the notes of a distant piano. Those distinctive, ethereal, haunting frequencies that she had spent so much of her life unraveling and riding on the wave of. It was coming from downstairs.

She followed the sound, gently placing one foot after the other on the hard stone steps. When she made it down to the parlor, her ears drew her closer to the piano. Yet there was no one playing it, no one human anyway. Again, it was a cat who was making the music.

"Wixby!" Hannah ran toward the piano.

He turned, his deep round eyes filled with knowing and joy at her arrival.

She sat down next to him as he continued to play. She knew this song. It was in the depths of her soul like a fogged-out memory. It was so close that her mind could almost grasp it, but so far away she couldn't hold onto it.

"I know this," she proclaimed, trying to will her mind into remembering the relevance. It was a specific repetition of notes that, when played together, resonated in such a way that in and of itself it effected change.

As Wixby extended his front legs playing the notes with his paws, Hannah heard an audible pop. It was the bench they sat on. Hannah stood up and picked up Wixby. He was soft and cuddly.

Once she stood, she could see that the bench held a secret compartment that closed with a latch. But the latch had popped open. Hannah placed her hand on the bench and slowly opened the lid. Her eyes were met with a large silver book titled *Eochair Airgid* in an ancient script font. She grasped the book and pulled it out. It too had a lock on it.

"Play those notes again," she told Wixby, closing the bench and setting him back down.

As Wixby played, the sequence rang through Hannah's mind and heart. As the vibrational frequency of the sound rippled through the room, she felt the lock to the book pop open.

"It's the music!" she exclaimed. "It's opening the locks!" Her heart leapt with extra tiny beats at the realization. "What is this song? How do you know it?"

"I saw Jewelia play it..." Wixby said matter-of-factly, pausing dramatically before adding, "when I traveled back in time."

"When you what?" Hannah asked, the book nearly falling from her hands. Was this what Madame Morgan had told her about?

"It was an accident, really," Wixby sheepishly began. He turned from the keys and sat up, facing Hannah. "It was a cold night and there was a huge thunderstorm. It arrived so fast, without warning. I wanted to get out of the rain, but the manor was too far away for me to reach it. I sought refuge in a large pumpkin in the patch. It must have been four times my size, and it was dank and dewy. The stem had somehow become rotted and fallen away, leaving a craggy hole in the top. When I jumped in, there was a grand flash of the brightest bolt of lightning I'd ever seen. I squeezed my eyes shut and held my breath, and the entire pumpkin filled with an intense glow, streaming bright as sunlight from the inside out like a lighthouse lantern. Then there was a bone-shaking rumble that knocked me around the pumpkin. I was terrified and my fur was standing on end. Then suddenly the rain and thunder stopped and the bright light was gone. I jumped out and ran through the patch as fast as my furry paws could take me, back toward the manor. But when I got there everything was different." His whiskers started to curve downwards and his tail twitched harder as he remembered his confusion of that night.

"Different, how?" Hanna asked. She started to pet Wixby down his back, gently caressing his fur.

"It was like it was another moment, another day. I saw Jewelia playing the piano, and she was playing this song. But she was younger, much younger than I had ever seen her. It has stayed with me all of this time. I just can't get it out of my head." Wixby seemed like he might be questioning his own experience.

"So you really did time travel...in a pumpkin," Hannah summarized for him.

"I suppose I did!"

"So how did you get back?" Hannah asked.

"The pumpkin, of course." Wixby flapped his tail on the bench.

As Hannah held the large silver book, she noticed that hanging off the side was a large silver tassel attached to a bookmark wedged between the pages. The bookmark was shaped like a key. She thought again of her dream of Abernathy and how he had given her a key. On the bookmark was a symbol with three letters: AGB.

"Are those initials?" Wixby asked. "Someone's name?"

Hannah stared at the bookmark. These were the letters on the key Abernathy had given her, which had unlocked the ancient bookshelf in her other dream. She then felt the parting of a veil in a dark corner of her mind. A remembering flooded her thoughts.

"Why didn't I see this before? Any musician worth their salt can recognize this! AGB!" Hannah exclaimed as the veritable light bulb glowed above her head, the clarity streaming through her mind. The letters weren't initials at all. They were musical notes! The notes on the key bookmark and the notes in Wixby's song were one and the same. They were both some sort of vibrational code, whose frequency resonated in such a way that secrets could be unlocked.

CHAPTER TWENTY-ONE

THE KEY

Hannah awoke again, and could sense it was day-light through her closed eyelids. But as she crossed over the barrier between the sleeping and the waking world, she paused for a minute in the middle world, the world between dreaming and waking. She dwelt there, soaking it in. Where had she just been? What had she just been doing? She had seen Wixby again, but what had he told her? She clung desperately to the dream memory as it quickly started to fade, faster and faster like a thought bubble popping into thin air.

It was the piano. Hannah lay as still as possible. She feared if she moved her limbs, the additional blood flow would somehow purge the memory she so longed to retain.

Wixby had appeared to her again, but what happened this time?

The piano...words echoed in her mind like they were delivered to her on a gentle breeze down a long dark corridor.

As she concentrated, she remembered Wixby play-ing the piano again, and that he had revealed to her a song that he discovered Jewelia playing when he had time traveled in a pumpkin. The dream was still fading fast, the details fuzzy, but she could hear the notes ringing in her ears. There had been a large silver book, but what was it and why hadn't she looked in it? She knew if she could get to the piano fast enough, she could play the song.

She quickly got up and ran down the hallway, continuing down the stairs at a fast clip. As she got closer to the piano her fingers began to tremble, alight with a buzzing energy. She sat down swiftly on the bench. As she began to play, she again heard Madame Morgan say, *it is time for you to align yourself with the frequencies of the island.*

When she thought of frequencies, Hannah thought of music. Perhaps by playing this song, which seemed to be somehow intertwined with Aunt Jewelia and her family lineage, she would then somehow step into the alignment Madame Morgan had spoken of.

As she played, she marveled how the song was unlike anything she had ever heard before, but at the same time was familiar. It was discovering and remembering all at once. Her fingers led the way, her heart warming and her mind quieting, as if concentration had no place in this activity. It was flow, and only that. The music channeled through her, carrying her away from the manor into a different space. She didn't have to think about it. The synergy between her nimble fingers and her intuitive ears was a long-established connection. There was a flow between them that didn't require planning, measuring, or calculating. She knew the notes and the notes knew her. As she translated the ethereal song from her mind's eye to her hands, it poured out of her in a smooth ocean of harmony. The frequencies rang out like a bell had been struck, and her body tingled and shimmered with the sensation.

In her mind's eye, Hannah began to see images. Were they memories, or were they experiences happening right now? She wasn't sure how to distinguish between them. But she followed the vision. The vision was of water—not above water, but below. Murky depths rippled in her mind. It was calm and dark, undulating with the flow of the chords and keys. Moving like a wave as they synchronized, carrying her further and further away.

When she played the last note of her dream song, she felt a pop come from underneath her.

It was the bench she was sitting on. It had pushed up against her, rising her off it. There was a latch on the bench that had popped open. It struck her like a bolt of lightning—this was in her dream! The music was a code. A combination that, when vibrating at the right frequency, had the ability to unhinge and unlock that which was hidden.

Hannah turned around to face the bench and opened the secret compartment. Her eyes widened at what she saw.

Chapter Twenty-Two

THE ISLAND

S he felt a cool breeze surround her. It was the chill she had felt before. It started near her lower back and rose up her right side, then crept like ice on a windowpane up her right shoulder, up her neck past her ear, and lifted through her hair to the crown of her head. She knew this chill now like an old friend, like a comforting signal from the beyond that she was on the right track, heading in the right direction, following the right path.

The item inside the bench was not a book but an old photo. Hannah stood still and stared at it, her breath held in her lungs unconsciously. It was a very old photo, the edges frayed, marred with creases, the sepia tones dulling the contrast it once had. She brought it up to her eyes for a closer look. It looked like some sort of an aerial shot. At the bottom she could make out some nearly faded script font that read

Maple Hollow, 1888

As she continued to stare at the photo, Hannah's eyes began to alternate between focusing and glazing over in a way that meant she wasn't looking at it at all. Then she realized what she was looking at.

It was in fact the island she stood on, the one her aunt lived on, the mysterious island that had called to her. But it was also something else. The island was shaped like a key. The top, where Skye Manor was, was rounded in a circle, the house at the center, with water all around it and large maple trees encircling the manor. The road to and through the center of town ran down the long portion of the key, each notch of the teeth of the key featuring a small side street of the town where the villagers lived.

Hannah pulled out her phone, opened up the translator and typed in *Eochair Airgid*. It was Irish for "silver key." Abernathy had gifted her a key. The island was a key. How did it fit? Then she began to compile all the times since this adventure began that she had seen a key. The letter from her aunt had a small key symbol in the wax seal, and Jewelia had told her to *discover the key*. When she arrived at the manor that first night in the car with Old Man Adams, she had seen a key etched into the iron gates at the entrance to the grounds. In the great hall, there was a large wall of keys. In her dream about the lighthouse, the compass was engraved with a skeleton key. The key in her dream with three letters on it had unlocked the bookshelf. In her dream about Wixby, she had seen a bookmark shaped like a key. And the frequencies of the notes displayed on the keys in her dreams had just opened the piano bench.

Hannah realized that the island itself was a key. It was the key to saving her aunt. All the synchronicities and signs had led her to this realization. But now that she had discovered the key, how could she harness its energy to unlock the mystery and find her aunt?

Hannah spent that afternoon combing the shores of Maple Hollow. Now that she had seen it from above, she was even more curious to see it in person. In some parts of the island, the shore was impassable, filled with cliffs or large craggy rocks strewn about from the wild waves of storms past. In other parts, she could easily walk along the sandy shore unobstructed. She had taken off her shoes, burying her toes in the sand. As she walked, her eyes indexed every inch that crossed her path, scouring the shore for any clue, any sign of her aunt. She listened intently to the sounds of the shore, the birds that flew overhead, and the ebb and flo of the waves. Eventually she had checked every part of the shore. The sun began to sink below the horizon as she stood alone, staring out across the sea. She closed her eyes, and in her mind and heart she asked for guidance. The sea responded with a comforting mist that delicately coated her face and hair. She was so close to finding the answer, unlocking the mystery of the island.

T hat night Hannah dreamed she was a little girl again. She had believed in magick then. The mundane encroachments of adult life had not yet tarnished her mind. Her heart was filled with youthful exuberance and wonder.

It was winter and cold. She was walking to catch her bus to school. As she walked, she dropped one of her school books. When she did, the string on her gray mitten snapped, the force of the book severing the connection.

Her hand slipped out of the mitten, the harsh wind cold against her skin. She wasn't concerned about the book; in fact, she left it behind. She kept walking, despite her hand feeling icy and exposed.

Suddenly it was summer. Hannah stood in a glowing golden field of wheat and flowers. The sun shone high in the sky and the warmth filled her whole body. As she pranced through the field, from her pocket she pulled out the mitten with the string. The mitten began to float in the air, as if it was a feather taken up by the wind. It floated higher and higher, growing as it rose up, larger and larger. When she looked up toward the sky, she saw it was no longer a mitten at all.

It was now a large kite, and it was no longer gray but had taken on a beautiful butterfly shape. Sprouting from the center was a cheery plum-magenta color. The wings were a beautiful lilac, their edges tipped in a deep lavender and violet like the sea at sunset.

Hannah felt light and free, the wind blowing gently in her hair, the sun warming her skin. The kite glistened across the sky as she skipped, her heart light and full.

CHAPTER TWENTY-THREE

THE CAFÉ

OCTOBER 30, 2007

H annah awoke filled with excitement, it was the first day of the annual Halloween Hollow and she was anxious to get to town to soak in the sounds and sights.

She rode out from the manor, found a spot to park her bike in town, and strolled along the sidewalk down the main street that was lined on both sides with bright orange pumpkins. Displays of orange chrysanthemums, pomegranates, winter berries, apples, and acorns hung in festive baskets from the quaint lamp posts. Tourists had descended on the village, filling every retail spot chock-full of people.

She spent the morning perusing the craft booths at the farmer's market, breathing in the wafting smells of cinnamon and cloves that floated in the air and sampling the scrumptious festival goodies. Children bobbed for apples, chased each other through corn mazes, and played amongst the multitude of harvest games while their parents picked out costumes for the big event. In the afternoon, she helped Morgan and Ashlin prepare the Haunt festivities for Halloween day. A large feast was being held in the center of town and everyone was invited.

It was early evening. Hannah's stomach was rumbling, so she decided to pop in the Dishwasher Café. As she entered, the sounds of clanking silverware on dishes echoed in the small space. The dining room was jammed full. There was a din of conversation, sparkling with occasional laughter and the squeaking chairs on the hard floor as people finished their dinners and departed.

"Good evening, ma'am, how may I assist you?" the host graciously asked, leaning behind the lectern next to the door.

"Table for one, please," Hannah answered.

"Right this way." The host led her through the maze of tiny tables and chairs toward the back. "Here we are," he said in a pleasant tone as he pulled out the chair for her and placed the menu on the table.

"Thanks," Hannah said as she sat down in the knobby wooden chair and adjusted to her surroundings.

"Your server will be right with you." The host disappeared back through the maze of tables toward the front of the café.

From where she was sitting, Hannah could see into the kitchen. It was filled with cooks rushing about their choreographed duties. As she watched, she noticed one cook in particular didn't seem friendly with the other cooks. He was tall and muscular, with a thick red beard and tattooed arms.

A slim middle-aged woman approached the table. "Welcome to the Dishwasher, I will be your server tonight. Let me know if you have any questions about the menu. Are you ready to order?"

Hannah studied the oversized menu. It was approachable, with lots of variety. She opted for the wood fired pizza, adding some unusual toppings to keep it interesting. Without writing anything down, the waitress acknowledged her order and disappeared into the kitchen.

Hannah took out her phone and continued her research about keys and their symbolism. A short time later, her pizza arrived. By this point she was so hungry she literally inhaled it. Her belly felt swollen with indigestion moments before she took her last bite.

"Will there be anything else?" the waitress asked, arriving with the check in hand.

"That was more than enough," Hannah replied. "Thank you."

She knew she had eaten too much, but now the only thing to do was walk it off. As she exited the café there was only a sliver of sunset left on the horizon. From this spot in Maple Hollow there was a fabulous view of the sea. As Hannah admired the setting sun, she noticed that the search boats were still circling the island looking for her aunt.

She walked with her bike for a while, but when her face began to feel flush, she decided to ride the rest of the way back to the manor. Perhaps it was the humidity, her exertion, or all the sweets from the festival that was making her feel so lousy. She made it back to the manor, but as soon as she got inside, she ran immediately to the bathroom.

She approached the sink and fumbled for the cold knob. As water began to flood out of the faucet, she cupped her hands under the stream and splashed pools of water on her face. She felt so hot, overly hot for a cool autumn evening. As she looked up from the sink, she suddenly felt very dizzy. The lights and ceiling swirled and her vision blurred. Her knees weakened, her body swayed, and then she collapsed. Everything went black.

Hannah lay on the floor of the bathroom. The water still ran fast in the sink.

I t was night. The moon was huge, like a planet about to have a collision with earth. Bats circled in a dance across the sky. Everything was coated with a greenish-blue hue. The trees were barren, having lost their leaves, only the scratchy raw fortitude of layered bark remaining. Hannah was surrounded by pumpkins and ancient, crumbling tombstones with illegible messages.

The pumpkins weren't fertile, though. They were rotting, their flesh beginning to squish under their moldy weight. There was a tall wrought-iron fence around the area she stood in. Its peaks reached high up into the sky, scratching the clouds. Each section of the fence had an ornate knotwork scroll on it, crested at the top with a spirally column that cast an ominous shadow on the ground. Bright lanterns glowed from the tops of the posts connecting the fence. Flickering, the lights illuminated the slow creeping fog, which now hung close to the ground, filling the spaces between the pumpkins and the stone tombstones. All of the pumpkins had been carved into jack-o'-lanterns bearing terrifying and ominous faces, flames flickering inside them.

Hannah felt a sick feeling, a foreboding feeling in the pit of her stomach. She was in a place of death. There was no life here. The vines were not green and thriving, not pulsing with life. Instead, they were shriveled up and gray, all the life sucked out of them. But it wasn't just the end of the season. It was more nefarious than that. She felt a negative presence; something was not right.

She heard a bell tolling in the distance and felt a panic sweep over her. The bell echoed across the land, channeling a foreboding message. She looked down at her feet—they were stuck, sucked into the mucky quicksand. She felt the tingle of something cold on her feet. It was a slow river of a thick black substance that was flowing closer to her, beginning to cover her feet and then her ankles. It flowed thicker and faster, rising up to her knees, then her thighs. She was sinking in it, her panic rising with each inch that enveloped her.

Her head swooned as a feeling of weakness came over her. She could not escape. She knew she was going to be consumed by it. She took in one last gulp of air, surrendered to the inevitability, and faced the blackness.

Chapter Twenty-Four

THE POISON

With a loud gasp, Hannah awoke. She was lying in bed, the covers tucked in around her neck. As she came back to consciousness, the feeling of doom she'd had in the dream followed her. Her stomach growled and knotted as she attempted to sit up. She had passed out, she was sick, something had happened to her—but what? She was in her bed now, but how did she get here?

Old Man Adams appeared at the doorway. "There you are," he said cheerfully. "I thought we had lost you,"

"What happened?" Hannah rubbed her hand through her hair.

"Well, as far as I can tell, you had a bad case of food poisoning. According to the family physician, that is. Glad he makes house calls."

"How did you find me? How did you know?" Hannah asked, confused.

"I came over to feed Midnight and heard the water running upstairs. When I yelled for you and there was no answer, I came up and found you."

Hannah had never had food poisoning before, but she wasn't sure that was all there was to it.

"Was it the pizza?" Hannah thought out loud, remembering her dinner at the Dishwasher Café.

"I'd stay away from it for a while, just in case," Adams added. He patted her shoulder in a reassuring way, as if the solution was quite simple.

"Right," Hannah echoed. Was her illness just a coincidence, or something more?

Chapter Twenty-Five

THE MOON

L ater that evening, Hannah lay in her bed by the open window and listened to the sounds of the night. The loud cadence of an owl's nocturnal song reached her ears. She listened in her stillness, attempting to decipher each individual sound. Out the window she could see bright twinkling stars overhead and the waning moon. It had been full for three days and was now nearly half shadow and half light.

Hannah thought about the phases of the moon, the celestial dance that played out across the sky every month. As she stared at the waning gibbous moon, she realized that the moon was teaching her all the time. Sometimes we stand in our brightness, sometimes we sit in our darkness, but at all times we must balance both sides of ourselves.

When she was unconsciousness from the food poisoning, she had gone deep into shadow. Now she had to emerge from that shadow, drawing on the light inside her. She had to continue to illuminate the path to her aunt; much like the moon as its illumination grows, she must light the way back to a reality, one in which she and Jewelia could exist together, one where they did not hide from the darkness, but also where they would not get lost forever. She knew it was a delicate balance.

Hannah had always felt the power of the moon when it was full, but she had never given much thought to the other phases, or what the moon's energy or power might be at other times of the month. She knew there was a connection between her body and the moon, that they did have a cycle that seemed to correspond. She knew it must all tie together.

Hannah loved to get lost in ideas about why we are here, who else is out there, and what else is possible. She relaxed into these deep existential thoughts, wondering about the universe, the planets, and the galaxies. Her curiosity was again like it was when she was a child. As she gazed out the window, she felt an invisible curtain lifting and the universe waving her in, inviting her to indulge her inner world of wonder.

Halloween was tomorrow night. The day when the veil was thinnest was upon them. She would harness this special time with her inner wisdom.

Her aunt was relying on her. The whole fate of Maple Hollow, and maybe the world, could very well depend on her.

Chapter Twenty-Six

THE VEIL

October 31, 2007

W hen Hannah awoke on Halloween morning, it was still dark outside. It felt as if night was going to continue and no day was coming. She rolled out of her bed and walked to the window that overlooked the pumpkin patch, and beyond it, the sea. There was a dense fog that had settled over the patch and grounds, its shadowy cloud making the whole scene appear to be floating in a grand sky castle.

Tonight was the night. The night of all nights. The time when other worlds were closest. The day when she would be most able to find and save her aunt.

She'd learned so much while being in Maple Hollow. She had shaken off the familiar feelings of inadequacy and insecurity that often lurked nearby, an unwelcome but familiar shade. She was choosing to listen to her new inner voice: *You know you can do this, you already know what you need to do. Your aunt needs you. This is your calling.*

Hannah snapped out of her trance. She hurriedly gathered her clothes and bag and left the bedroom, running down the staircase, through to the foyer, and straight outside toward the pumpkin patch.

As she ran, she felt the dewy air coat her skin and hair. Her lungs felt fresh and new as she submerged herself into the fog. She was running blindly now, letting her feet lead her on a path she knew not where.

She stopped suddenly, her heart pounding. She looked down and saw that she was standing, barefoot, in the pumpkin patch, and the vines of the patch were intertwining around her feet and ankles. She began to feel an intense chill, but it wasn't from the air. It was the tingly connectedness that she only felt when she was aligned, on the right track, in the flow, not afraid, not doubting, trusting her path and her connection.

She instinctively knew that this was where she should be this morning. This patch was the answer, as it always had been. She'd known this ever since she first had the dream, although it hadn't made sense at the time. The pumpkin patch was a network, not just in her dream, but multi-dimensionally, beyond space and time, beyond waking and sleeping, beyond the world she had previously known. Today it would all come together, it would all make sense. She would no longer harbor doubts about her ability, her calling, her purpose. She would embrace an inner knowing that did not have to be proven, endorsed, quantified, sanctioned, certified, allowed, or condoned. It didn't have to be, because it already was. It existed across planes of existence she couldn't previously have fathomed, between spaces others refused to notice, above and below all the mundane, the expected, the correct, the limitations of illusory reality.

Her birthright was as a Healer of the Hollow. Her portal the pumpkin patch. Her purpose was to guide lost souls who had succumbed to the false siren song of the Dream Haunters, convinced to stay asleep, coaxed to believe their own doubts, resigned to exist only in nightmares of their own devising. They were trapped within the depths of themselves. But she had a way out for them, a light in the darkness. Jewelia had been the lighthouse to so many, but something had happened to her vibration in the shadow of retrograde—Hannah knew her aunt must have been haunted by self-doubt and sapped of her energetic gifts.

But now she was here in Maple Hollow to restore Jewelia and take up the torch of the Healer. She had it within her to align herself with her true power. And she would do it tonight.

She looked around the pumpkin patch, at all the oversized pumpkins glowing in the soft dawn light, and decided to choose her portal. She selected a perfect pumpkin that lay near her feet, separating it from the vine. When she did so, she felt a tingling tickle, as if a spark of the current that flowed from the vines to the pumpkin was now entering her hands. The energy coursed through her as she rose from the patch, her arms wrapped around the heavy gourd.

The wind was blowing cool as the sun crested the horizon. Dry crackling leaves gathered into piles on their own, blown by the gentle hands of the wind. Hannah carried her pumpkin back to the manor. It was very heavy, and her upper back and shoulders ached as she clenched her muscles to support it. She went into the library and placed the pumpkin on a table closest to the door, Midnight following her closely.

Hannah located the squeaky floorboard, opened the trap door, and descended the spiral stairs. She gazed at the books she had run her fingers over a few days before. She was looking for the book about vortexes, which she believed could guide her in harnessing the pumpkin portal's power for herself. She pulled *Unraveling the Secrets of Island Vortexes: An Insider's Look* from the shelf, then turned back and headed upstairs to the library.

Retrieving *Spiritual Vortexes* from its shelf, she carried both books over to a comfortable chair that had a lamp conveniently placed next to it and settled in to read. The sun wafted gently through the slightly open window as if flowing through the ocean depths. She could hear the distant sound of the sea like a comforting white noise, the seagulls gently blending with the dewy wall of sound. She spent hours in the library getting lost in the magickal books. They taught her so much about the island and its energies. They spoke of the lore of ley lines and the mystical power these are able to channel. It was making sense.

So many people were struggling, trapped in their dreams by the Dream Haunters. It was time for her to stand at the precipice of power, the connecting points of all the magnetic forces and ley lines on the island, and open the magical portal of the dreamworld, passing through the interdimensional doorway of time and space to bring back those who are lost, healing their souls and vanquishing all doubt.

Hannah thought about how this Halloween was also the last night of Mercury retrograde. The power of retrograde was waning. At midnight, Mercury would go direct and retrograde would end. The Dream Haunters, she knew, had been using retrograde to their advantage. Aunt Jewelia's letter said she must open the portal by tonight. Tonight was Halloween: it was the moment when the veil between the worlds is the thinnest. She would defeat the Dream Haunters and find Jewelia tonight. She had to save her, or the Dream Haunters would win, and Jewelia would be missing forever.

Eventually Hannah decided she needed to clear her head to do things right. In every moment of stillness, there was an opportunity for a moment of clarity. And it was only in those delicate moments of nothing that there could be…something.

She left the library, stopped at the kitchen to grab some lunch, and walked outside, mounting her bike. She wasn't even sure where she was headed, but she knew she would find out best if she didn't ask, didn't overthink it, just went.

As she rode along the tree-lined streets of Maple Hollow, she passed the joyful chaos of Halloween Hollow in full swing. The tourists had descended on the village and were filling every sidewalk and café. They hopped from one activity to the next, taking in all the fall activities of the island. It was a time of celebration, dedication, and remembrance for all the townspeople. Everyone was preparing their festivities, gathering their harvest, making their feasts, and decorating their abodes. Children giddily ran in circles around each other, playing with their costumes, chattering about the corn mazes, and laughing on the hayrides.

Hannah had scarcely noticed how far into town she had gone when she looked up and realized she was standing in front of Madame Morgan's shop. But when she looked in the window, she saw that the shop was jammed-packed with tourists and Morgan was running about in a flurry attempting to tend to everyone's inquiries.

It was time for her to face this alone. She knew the task before her and what she was being called to do. The island was a key, the manor was a key, and there was a key to the mystery that had drawn her into this mysterious web. It was now time for her to unlock the mystery and free Jewelia once and for all. She hoped that the gray shadow of her childhood could also be unlocked, perhaps even banished. It was the turning of the year. She could find her own rebirth beyond it. She could harness the eternal cycle of the falling leaves, the inevitable death, and transform it into a new life, a rebirth, a new chapter. A chapter where she would be transformed as well.

Hannah swung her bike around and headed back to the manor, now at a quicker pace. She felt a sense of urgency to get back—there was little time left on the clock.

When she arrived at the manor, she ran to the library, grabbed the pumpkin off the table, and opened the trap door. She descended the stairs, placing each foot carefully on the precarious steps. She couldn't see her feet beyond the pumpkin and didn't want to be tripped by Midnight, who was, of course, close behind her.

When she reached the bottom of the stairs, she set down the pumpkin and peeled back the spine of the unmarked Celtic book to open the bookcase to the secret room beyond. The door creaked aside. She entered and placed her pumpkin on the table.

Hannah began lighting the various candles throughout the room, some sitting on tables, benches, and bookshelves, others tall in grand candlesticks and illuminating the ceiling. Once the room was aglow in a warm golden hue, she returned to the lectern and stood over the *Grimoire de Skye*. Her eyes scanned the

instructions for *Tairseach an Phuimcín*. It was now time
for her to tap the neural network. She must enter the
pumpkin portal and go to the dream dimension to save
her aunt. It was now or never.

Hannah sat down and called for Midnight to come
sit in her lap, which he did immediately. She grabbed
her phone, opened a translator app, and began typing
in each line on the page of instructions in the grimoire.

Closing her eyes, she began to center herself by
calming her breath. Her concentration deepened as
she focused on her breathing, slow and controlled: fully inhaling, holding it for a moment, then slowly exhal-
ing it out and holding it there, all the air having exited
her lungs. She sat in that stillness, the flames stoically
bearing witness—no flicker, no wind, just silence and
stillness. As her body calmed, so too did her mind and
spirit. She began to chant the translated words from
the ancestral book.

"I invoke now, that all my highest and brightest
guides surround me on this most sacred of days. This
night, when the veil to other dimensions is at its
thinnest. I invoke now, all ancestral power I carry in my
being and all energetic abilities that have lain latent
until now. Walk with me in the darkness, may the
portal be open. May the mysteries be unveiled. May
those who are trapped by the Dream Haunters be free
once more. So Mote It Be."

Hannah closed her eyes again and placed her hands
upon the pumpkin. She sat in stillness, following her
breath. She began to feel a chill, not from the basement, but rather from within herself. It started on her
right outer thigh and crept up her side to her back.
Then up her neck to the back of her head. Then to the
crown of her head.

Beneath her hands, she began to feel a vibration and heat emanating from the pumpkin. She stayed still, her arms extended, her hands on the pumpkin, as if she was channeling from a large crystal ball.

She felt as if she was holding her breath. In her mind's eye, she began to see water all around her and felt as if she had been plunged into an underwater world. It was deep, deep underwater, because she could not see sunrays coming through; in fact, she could see very little. She then realized that she could in fact breathe and didn't need to hold her breath, and that she could swim quite effortlessly through this cavernous aquarian world. She saw ahead of her a massive old ship. It was ornate, like a pirate ship, with beautifully carved spires.

As Hannah approached the ship, she noticed a dim light emanating from within. And she thought she heard a woman's voice. Hannah entered the ghost ship through an open window, past seaweed gently floating on water waves around the frame.

As she entered, she felt an incredible sadness come over her. She wasn't sure if these were her emotions or someone else's. But she felt sure someone else was trapped down here and she was meant to save her. Could it be Aunt Jewelia?

She swam around the hallways and into small rooms, checking all over the ship. Then she saw it: a purple cloud of glitter emanating from underneath a door.

Hannah approached. The door was enormous, wooden, and very heavy. She tried the handle but it was padlocked. On the door, which was carved out of wood, was also what appeared to be piano keys. It was almost as if a keyboard had been etched into the door itself. She extended her thin fingers toward the keys.

As she pressed down her pointer finger, she heard a tone ring out that sounded exactly like a piano. She marveled at how this could be possible, but instinctively placed her other fingers on the rest of the keys.

She realized at that moment that although she knew that the notes she needed to play were AGB, she didn't know which octave to play AGB in to achieve the correct frequencies. She closed her eyes and listened to the whispers in her soul. Following her intuition, she played the first note, A, in the fourth octave. In her mind's eye, she pictured the four statues that stood watch over the family hearth at the manor, and then chose G in the fourth octave as the next note. Lastly, she had to select the B note, but what should she pick? She thought about all the cats that had guided her along the way, her treasured Mystera and the cats of Maple Hollow: Midnight, Merlin, Milu, and Wixby. She played the B note in the fifth octave.

As soon as she did so, the keyboard began to rotate back onto itself and slid to the right, revealing yet another lock. Hannah thought of the key she'd received in her dream from Abernathy the turtle. No sooner had she thought of it than it appeared in her hand. It was a large, ornate silver key. Without thinking, just feeling and following her gut, Hannah inserted the key into the lock of the ship door. The moment the key touched, a bright white light began to issue forth from it. It was so bright she almost had to look away. As she turned the key, the door creaked open and light overtook the entire doorway, flooding both her and the ocean around her with the bright white light.

She'd never met her aunt, but she had an instinctual feeling she was here. "Jewelia?"

As she said this, her aunt emerged into being in the light, her green eyes meeting Hannah's, glowing like a vibrant fire. An expression of complete relief and profound joy was on her face. Hannah reached out a hand, as did her aunt.

As their fingertips touched, the ship filled with a tornado of violet swirling crystalline energy. It raced around, surrounding them until Hannah could see nothing else. Her heart burst with a feeling of immense power, gratitude, and light.

Within seconds, she was back in the secret room and opened her eyes. Her hands were still on the pumpkin, except now the pumpkin had been carved. Etched through its rind was a *cló aisling,* the ghostly ship of Jewelia's captivity in the depths of the ocean.

At that moment, Hannah heard a thud outside the door. Midnight jumped from her lap and was standing alertly, meowing, twitching his tail and looking upward at the heavy door.

Who else knew about the trapdoor in the library and the secret stairway? Could it be Old Man Adams? Hannah cautiously walked toward the door. Her hands grasped the handle. A long, slow creaking sound filled the room and a low fog crawled along the floor. She stared into the darkness.

Chapter Twenty-Seven

THE REUNION

J ewelia slowly walked toward Hannah through the fog. She looked just like she did in the painting at the top of the grand staircase, except this time she was real, in the flesh, her earthly body now returned to this time and space, the earthly plane that Hannah existed in. She was no longer a prisoner of the murky depths of her dream, trapped in the ghostly ship of her mind. She was no longer surrounded by the deep fears that had seized her breath, drowning her, suspending her in a floating death in the dark. Hannah had freed her, released her from her dark servitude. The pumpkin bore the cryptic engraving of her former dwelling, the nightmare she had been trapped in.

"Hannah?" Jewelia asked, her eyes lighting up.

"Aunt Jewelia?" Hannah answered, a flurry of unbelieving surprise and relief filling her chest.

"Yes, it's me," Jewelia said, opening her arms to her niece. They embraced in relief. "Thank you! I didn't think you'd be able to find me," she whispered, pulling back to gaze with joy at Hannah. "I knew the Dream Haunters were tracking me, and I tried everything to reverse it, but the retrograde was working against me.

My reversal magick didn't work and I thought I would be trapped forever. How did you know where to find me?"

Hannah reached into her pocket and pulled out the folded letter. When Jewelia saw her writing on the envelope, recognition flashed across on her face. "The letter!" she exclaimed. "I had forgotten about that! I'm so glad it reached you."

"I didn't even know you, and I almost didn't come," Hannah started to explain, "but there was something calling me to Maple Hollow. I was having dreams I couldn't explain. About pumpkin patches!"

Jewelia smiled. "Of course you were," she said, still in that knowing tone.

Hannah had been drawn to the island. It was, after all, her time to discover her true calling. We all have those moments in life where we hear the call. The call to take a detour, to go down the unknown road of uncertainty. To depart from the path we are on and follow another voice that, although sometimes subtle, is also quite stubborn in its pursuit of us. The urgency one cannot ignore and the undertow of curiosity despite the danger.

As they stood holding hands, gazing into each other's eyes and basking in the relief of their re-union, Midnight swirled between their ankles, his tail wrapping to and fro in feline greeting.

"Midnight, my love," Jewelia said, picking him up and holding him close to her heart.

They then all heard something. It was quiet at first, like a shuffled footstep, but becoming louder. Suddenly, a green trail of light slithered down the spiral staircase and began to flood the room. The candles that had surrounded them blew out and an eerie foreboding filled the air. Someone was down there with them.

Jewelia and Hannah stood still as statues. Then she showed herself. It was Norma Nyx, the so-called detective.

She lurched toward Jewelia, her normally perfectly coiffed hair coming unhinged from her bun and her face contorted in frustration and rage at Jewelia's escape. Jewelia's expression quickly turned from one of gratitude and peace to rage and resentment. A strong wave of anger, self-protectiveness, and revolt washed over her face. Norma was reaching for her neck, attempting to choke her, attempting to squeeze the earthly breath and life force out of her.

At first Jewelia succumbed to the choking, her subconscious and conscious minds at war over whether she was still trapped under the sea and her lungs were filling with water, leaving no room for even a drop of air. Her brain tried to work it out but her body began to freeze, her lungs iced over in her chest, unable to expand. Her face began to gray.

It all happened in an instant. Hannah was so shocked that she literally felt like she was floating in the room above it all, observing, unable to actually participate or do anything about the situation.

Norma had been unable to keep Jewelia trapped in her nightmare. She was obviously furious that she had failed and now desperately trying to destroy her another way. She was driven to deactivate Jewelia's power, dull her senses, and remove her from this existence.

Initially, it seemed to be working. Despite how angry she looked, Jewelia appeared to be caught in a trance between worlds—the world of her dream that had trapped her, and the world where Hannah had saved her. She seemingly had two choices: she could stay here, in this physical reality above water where she had agency and hope, or she could allow Norma to send her back below the sea, to the depths of her doubt, paralyzing fear, and inaction. She would be lost in the stillness, immobile, unfulfilled, unrealized.

At that moment, Midnight jumped onto Norma's back, sinking his sharp claws into her spine. Norma yelped and her grip gave way. She fell to the floor, her back like a stiff board, her nerves somehow paralyzed. Jewelia staggered toward the lectern and clutched it as her face began to warm, her complexion gaining a peachy glow as the blood returned to it, her eyes blinking as she roused herself from the waking dream dimension that Norma had nearly forced her into. She looked first at Hannah and then at Norma on the ground.

"Thank you, my love," she whispered to Midnight, scooping him up. Her gaze returned to Norma's stiff body. "It is time to banish you, Dream Haunter," she declared. "Hannah, let's prepare."

Hannah looked at her aunt. "Prepare how?"

"Gather the candles and put them in a circle around her body. Any size candle will do. Grab as many as you can, quickly now!" Jewelia instructed.

Norma remained motionless on the cold basement floor, her arms still outstretched. Hannah raced to the shelves and tables to get the candles, many of which were still lit. Her hands got coated with dripping wax as she hurriedly placed the candles, one by one, around Norma's body. For the wicks that were not lit, she fetched long matches from a large black vase and struck them on its exterior to light each wick in order. She wasn't sure what she was doing, exactly, but it seemed that Jewelia was allowing her to follow her instincts. The actions were flowing from her in a way that made her think perhaps she had done this before. Maybe she was not a stranger to banishment rituals. It was as if her ancestral knowledge was coming to the fore, rising out of the ether and coming to her aid at this pivotal moment.

Jewelia was pacing around Norma's motionless body. "We will need another pumpkin!" she said urgently, her eyes flashing. "Run now, Hannah, to the patch, as fast as you can."

Hannah's heart quickened. She turned like a tornado toward the door. It was a blur as she ran, first up the spiral stairway long and dark, then through the library and the shadowy hallway, out the back door of the manor into the crisp evening air. She ran toward the patch, faster and faster down the long hedge-lined path.

Suddenly, a hand reached out from behind a hedge and grabbed her arm. She was jerked to the ground, crashing to the hard soil on her elbows and knees. She looked up and saw, hovering over her, the large dark shadow of a man. He was much taller and stronger than she was, and he held a heavy metal shovel in his hand.

"I've been waiting for you," he said darkly. "You won't get away with this. You can't defeat us."

It was then that Hannah realized who it was—it was the cook with the red beard, the one working at the Dishwasher Café the night she'd been poisoned. She also realized that she'd seen the tattoo on his arm somewhere before—was it on the luggage tag in the airport when she'd departed for Maple Hollow? Yes, it was a circle with a triangle and a snake inside.

She knew in her bones this "person" was Quint Maytox, a Dream Haunter, part of the same secret society as Norma. They knew about her power, her legacy, her family. They were here to stop her, to stop Jewelia. They had wanted to keep Jewelia trapped forever, but now that Hannah had freed her, they were desperate to complete the plan.

Chapter Twenty-Eight

THE PUMPKIN PATCH

"I am a Dream Haunter," Quint proclaimed, sneering down at Hannah. "I know your darkest fears. You can't hide from me. I know everything about you," he added as he inched closer to her, wielding the shovel over his head.

Hannah squirmed on the ground, backing up each time he stepped closer.

"I know your darkness," he continued, "and I will trap you there forever." He swung the shovel toward her.

Hannah's instincts kicked in and she raised her arm in defense. At that exact moment, the Dream Haunter's shovel met resistance from another shovel. It was Old Man Adams, come to save her! The two shovels met with a loud clang. The two men grappled, their shovels jousting as they attempted to block and push each other down.

"Not you, Adams," Quint yelled. "You can't defeat me!" His strong arms exerted force over Adams' older frame. "Your time has passed, Old Man," he barked, as if his negativity would influence Old Man Adams into believing his words and surrender.

Adams' arms began to shake. Hannah couldn't move, looking up in shock at the shadow of the two men battling above her. At that moment, Midnight came running from behind the bushes and, with a loud forceful meow, ran between the Dream Haunter's legs and around his feet, just enough to destabilize and distract him. He faltered, and when he did, Old Man Adams raised his shovel above his head and delivered a mighty blow to his neck, knocking him to the ground. Quint's face smashed into the moist dirt. He was knocked out cold.

Old Man Adams took a breath. "Are you okay?" He stretched out his hand to Hannah.

"Yes, thank you." She stood up, still reeling from what had just happened. "Aunt Jewelia...she's come back!"

"What?" Adams yelled in surprise. "How?" he continued, as Hannah started to wipe the dirt from her clothes.

"No time to explain right now," she replied, remembering the mission she'd been sent on by her aunt, that she must get an additional pumpkin to banish Norma. "She's in danger and needs help." The stress of having left Jewelia alone with Norma was growing into a creeping fear of losing her aunt once more.

"What can I do?" Old Man Adams asked.

"We need a pumpkin. Meet me in the library!" Hannah ordered, then asked quickly, "you know about the trap door, right?"

Old Man Adams nodded. "Of course." He turned as fast as the wind and ran into the patch.

Hannah sprinted back toward the manor. She knew she had to get back before Norma woke. They had to banish both Dream Haunters while they were unconscious.

As she ran, she reminded herself that the Dream Haunters were not humans. Although they could stand and walk between worlds, they were actually manifested figments of people's imagination. They were representations, in human form, of people's greatest doubts and fears. Leveraging the power of Mercury retrograde, they were here to trap each dreamer in their worst nightmare. They existed by appealing to human weaknesses. They trapped people in the dark shadows of their own minds and convinced them to give in. The cook had tried to poison her and now was trying to make her and Old Man Adams believe they could never win against him. It wasn't just their physical strength he challenged, but their mental strength as well. Dream Haunters embodied the darker side of existence.

Not only had Hannah doubted her worth for so long, but Aunt Jewelia, upholding her traditions and ways, had started to feel alone and weakened in her power. Like so many people, they had each become trapped inside their own doubts. As if on a hamster wheel, they felt the passage of time and grew tired, not realizing they were stuck in a loop. A loop of lower vibration, negativity, and doubt that spread into a creeping shadow, occluding every spark of inspiration or fleeting sense of possibility they might have.

But once Hannah recognized that she was on that wheel, she could see the larger picture. She could finally break through the false illusion, freeing herself to roll beyond its limits. She was still gaining momentum and speed, propelled beyond the limitations she'd previously accepted for herself.

Madame Morgan had told her she was a Healer, and now she understood. She knew the Ferris wheel of her existence was about to roll in a different direction.

As she pulled up the trap door in the library, Hannah imagined her Ferris wheel, the hamster wheel, beginning to form the shape of a large pumpkin. The pumpkin was her wheel now, unfettered. It powered her potential, her new path, her new direction in life, destabilized and free. She had seen how a pumpkin removed from a patch took on a life of its own, even becoming an interdimensional portal for the work of the Healers.

Racing down the spiral stairs, Hannah wondered if they would need a pumpkin for the other Dream Haunter as well as for Norma. Would she have to get Jewelia and Norma into the pumpkin patch?

In the basement, she heard a crackling noise coming from behind the bookshelf. She'd left the secret door open, but now it was closed. She tried to pull on the books, but the door would not budge. Panic began to course through Hannah's body at the thought she could lose her aunt once more. Perhaps Norma had come to and closed the door, sealing them both inside so that no help could enter. What if Norma trapped Jewelia again and she got stuck in her nightmare forever?

Hannah's hands began to shake and sweat, her pulse throbbing now in her throat. She looked desperately for the book she'd used to enter the secret room—it was so hard to miss with its distinctive Celtic-patterned spine. Her eyes darted to and fro but she didn't see that book now at all! Could Norma have taken it and locked herself inside? How was she going to get the door open now that the book to get in was missing?

She heard Old Man Adams' voice from above. "I've got it, I've got it!" he yelled, his footsteps pounding across the library to the open trap door. His pace slowed as he arrived on the final step of the spiral staircase and saw Hannah standing in front of the closed bookshelf. He was grasping a gigantic pumpkin in his hands, breathing heavily and sweating from running with the heavy gourd.

"The book I need is gone," Hannah said desperately. "I don't know how to get in!"

"What do you mean?" he stammered.

"The book, the one I used before to get inside, it's not here, I can't find it!"

"What book?" Adams asked again, so confused.

"How else can we get inside?" Hannah demanded.

"Inside?" He looked even more confused.

Hannah realized that although Old Man Adams knew about the trapdoor and staircase, he didn't know about the secret room.

The key, a voice behind them said.

They both turned around but saw no one. Then they noticed a wisp of a gray tail pass around the corner at the top of the stairs.

"Who said that?" Hannah asked.

"It wasn't me," Adams replied, still gripping the enormous pumpkin.

In a flash, Hannah remembered the wall of keys in the great hall upstairs. Perhaps one of them would work to open the secret room. Maybe Jewelia had created an alternate way to open up the room in the event something happened to the book.

"The keys!" she shouted at Adams, bolting up the spiral stairs. As she crossed the foyer into the great hall, she heard the distant call of crows and owls, the sound reminding her that time was short.

Staring at the wall of keys, she felt dwarfed by the choices. There were so many—how could she know the right one to pick? Should she just start grabbing them all? How would she even reach the others? The ceiling was extremely high, so high that even the tallest ladder might not reach. She now could hardly contain her pounding heart.

Which key, which key? she repeated to herself as her eyes scanned all the different keys on the wall. Some had unique symbols on them she had never seen before. Others had numbers etched in their worn and ancient metal. As she scanned them, she also wondered where the lock was on that bookshelf, anyway. Some of the keys were the size of her arm. There was no way there was a keyhole that large that she would have missed.

At that moment, she heard a voice. It wasn't in the room around her. It was more inside her head. It was like a thought, but she recognized it as different, an inner voice. She remembered that when she first received the letter from her aunt, on the red wax seal of the envelope was the shape of a skeleton key. When she'd first arrived at the manor, the headlights from Old Man Adams' car had illuminated a key symbol on the gate to the property. In her dream of the lighthouse, there was a compass that bore the symbol of the skeleton key. And Abernathy the turtle had brought her a key unearthed from the bottom of the pond. Hannah then remembered the first time she dream-traveled, and how in her mind's eye she was holding a key, the same one Abernathy had given her. When she saved Aunt

Jewelia from her nightmare, she had used that same silver key.

Hannah's attention was drawn behind her. There was a fire crackling in the very large fireplace. She remembered reading that Samhain was an ancient Celtic fire festival. The fire was popping and dancing, but it was something more than fire. In the flames, she began to see a vision. As the sparks floated up into the chimney, disappearing in air, she began to see something much different than she'd ever seen in a fire before.

Calmness swept over Hannah. She felt a sense of being guided. She walked slowly toward the fire.

As she stood in front of the fireplace, the flames casting a warm glow over her body, she closed her eyes. In her mind's eye, she could see inside the secret room. She could see Aunt Jewelia. She envisioned Norma being consumed by the flames, her body evaporating instantaneously into thin air. It was as if she had combusted, however, not burned.

In that moment, Hannah knew Norma was gone.

She hurried back to the basement, but there was no sign of Old Man Adams. His pumpkin sat on the floor by the bookshelf, and now the door was open.

Aunt Jewelia was standing there, and there was no sign of Norma's body. "You did it, Hannah!" Jewelia exclaimed. "Well done!" She reached out to hug her niece.

"Really?" Hannah couldn't believe it. Had she truly banished Norma with the power of her mind?

"Norma's gone," Aunt Jewelia proclaimed. "You dissolved her back into the ether." She looked Hannah square in the eye. "As well as being a Dream Haunter, Norma was a shapeshifter. She only has power during Mercury retrograde and could only access this plane of existence because it coincided with Halloween. Tonight is the last night of retrograde, and you, Hannah, sent her back!"

"Oh my. Wow!" Hannah digested this. "But where is Old Man Adams?" she asked. "He brought a pumpkin. That other Dream Haunter attacked us outside and we barely got away. I was looking for a key in the fireplace room," she tried to explain, distractedly.

"Did you say Old Man Adams? That's what your father used to call him. I'll be so glad to see him again," Aunt Jewelia said happily. "Let's go find him. Don't you see, Hannah," she continued, "you stepped between the worlds and without even being present, helped me dissolve Norma. She is no longer on this plane and cannot hurt us."

"It was the fire in the fireplace," Hannah said thoughtfully. "I was looking everywhere for a key to this room, since the book I used before was gone. There were so many keys I wasn't sure which one would work. Then the fire drew me in. I started to see a vision, and a feeling swept over me that I no longer needed to look for a key."

"That, my love, is because *you* are the key," Jewelia said proudly. "The reason you're here, the reason you were drawn to Maple Hollow, is because you hold inside you the power to vanquish all the Dream Haunters. Their power is nothing compared to yours. You just needed to learn how to tap it." She patted Hannah's arm. "You've summoned the elements—earth, water, air, and fire—to help you. Do you remember how you used the earth, the pumpkin patch, the water, to save me from my nightmare? And the air when you played keys of music to free me? And now the fire, to destroy Norma."

"It all makes sense now, yes," Hannah said. "Let's go, we have one more job to do!" She flew back up the dark spiral stairway, Jewelia at her heels.

In tandem they ran through the foyer and out the back door of the manor toward the sea. A look of sheer determination was on Aunt Jewelia's face. She was back and was never going to be trapped again. In this moment, Hannah felt that same feeling in her soul. She had discovered something she never realized was within her. She had vanquished a Dream Haunter without really trying. She finally was part of a family, and now that she had this connection, she was never going back. They were in this together. Side by side, they ran to the pumpkin patch.

The pounding of their feet came to a sudden stop when Jewelia tripped. Hannah watched Jewelia fall head over heels into a deep dark hole in the ground. She heard her hit the bottom with a thud. Hearing footsteps behind her, she quickly ducked behind a tall bush. Quint had come to and was pushing a metal grate over the opening. He was closing off the hole, trapping Jewelia.

"NO!!! I will NOT be trapped again," Jewelia yelled at the Dream Haunter.

"I rule the night," Quint yelled through the grate, asserting his sheer intent to not relinquish his power.

"You do not, and you will not," Aunt Jewelia shouted back defiantly.

"There is no escaping me, you fools," Quint yelled down the hole. "I—" At that moment a shadow appeared behind Quint, and he collapsed to the ground.

It was Old Man Adams, the metal shovel in his hand once more. "It's over!" he yelled at the Dream Haunter, attempting to strike him again.

But Quint was not defeated. The two men struggled again, this time dropping their weapons and fighting with sheer force of will against one another. Quint delivered a final blow to Old Man Adams, knocking him out.

"I've got the keys," Quint said, holding the cast-iron manor keys tauntingly above the grate. "Now I rule the pumpkin patch," he said triumphantly. "I can do my will, as I wish, and rule you all!" He reached up and shook his arms at the wide-open sky, his madman silhouette shadowing the grave-like pit.

Hannah reached for her phone, quickly pulling up the photos she had taken of pages from the *Grimoire de Skye*.

"*Fill ar an Dorchadas!*" she shouted, stepping out from the safety of the bushes.

"Return to darkness!" Jewelia's voice rose from the hole.

"*Déantar aischéimniú,*" Hannah continued, pronouncing her bold exorcism with one hand holding her phone and the other stretched into the night air. As she read the mystical lines from her screen, smoke rose around her and an illuminated triangle formed between her and the ground. At each point of the triangle, through the smoke were glowing pairs of tiny cat eyes.

"Retrograde is done!" Hannah heard Jewelia's voice yell from the pit as she delivered her last lines of demolition.

With each phrase Hannah intoned, Quint became weaker and weaker. First he fell to his knees, then he began shaking and breaking apart until he was just one large cloud of negative energy cells bundled together. The glowing triangle shifted into a funnel of light, swirling faster and faster. As she spoke her final words, Quint disappeared into the ether.

Hannah ran to the edge of the hole. "Jewelia! Are you okay?!"

It was then that she saw two pairs of eyes staring back at her and realized it was not just Jewelia trapped in the hole, but Madame Morgan as well. As their eyes met, they found solace. The solace of a thousand years that every woman seeks. It was a certainty that despite the predicament they found themselves in, it was not the end for them.

"Morgan!" Hannah exclaimed.

"Hannah!" the two women shouted joyfully in return. "Yes, get us out of here!" Morgan's eyes were glowing bright, and she smiled ear to ear at the sight of Hannah.

"I've got you," Hannah told them. She stepped away from the hole, raised her arms in the air, and looked up at the now vividly bright sunset painted across the sky. The cold wind blew on the cornstalks, crows cawing in the distance, and bats circling overhead as the bright moon began to rise.

"*Múscail Fíniúnacha,*" Hannah roared, with all the vigor she could muster.

At that moment, a low rustling began. It was the earth breaking apart as all the vines of the pumpkin patch began to snake and swirl. She was awakening the vines. As she repeated the incantation twice more, the vines came to life, rapidly snaking down into the hole where Jewelia and Morgan were held captive. The vines wrapped around each woman's body, enveloping but not squeezing. It was a co-creation, a collaborative exchange. The vines then broke apart the grate and lifted them up out of the hole into the beautiful autumn sunset. Both of them gazed at the sky as they rose from their darkness. Once they reached ground level the vines released them, then wrapped around Old Man Adams as well, restoring him to health and awareness.

Hannah had summoned the power of the pumpkin patch to save them all. The wondrous vines held so much power and magick. So much compassion and force. Their energy was the energy of life. It could both give it and take it away. It was a power to be respected and revered.

"Thank you, Hannah," they all echoed. The three women embraced, exchanging hugs and reassuring words. Old Man Adams leaned on his shovel and smiled at them. The bats swirled overhead, dancing in the fantastical sunset. Midnight, Merlin, and Milu watched with wide eyes. They were all finally together. Hannah had come into alignment with her powers, and they were all safe at last.

Chapter Twenty-Nine

THE HOLLOW

"It's finally Samhain," Jewelia proclaimed as the sun sank into the horizon in a blinding blaze of purple and orange.

"The Halloween Hollow dinner should be ready," Morgan said, nodding and smiling. "It was pretty much all set before I was so unceremoniously snatched away."

"And I left the firewood at the door for the village bonfire," Old Man Adams said, winking.

"Then let's go, the village awaits us!" Aunt Jewelia said.

"Let's go celebrate!" Hannah agreed.

"I'll drive," Old Man Adams declared.

When they arrived in town, the streets were bustling with locals and visitors alike, all anticipating the festival's climactic event. Morgan had spent all day coordinating the feast preparation. As they gathered around the long, expansive tables set up along the main street of Maple Hollow, festival-goers mixed in at the tables amongst the villagers.

Children chased each other in circles around the tables, stopping to bob for apples and stuff sweet treats in their pockets. The crowd celebrated and indulged into the wee hours, sharing tales and smiles. Reunions of all sorts seemed to be sprouting up all around. Long-lost relatives and friends, it turned out, had returned from the ether as a result of Hannah's magick, their souls freed from the Mercury retrograde grip of the Dream Haunters.

"I meant to ask you," Jewelia said at one point, turning to Hannah, "how did you know to activate the vines to save us?"

"Well, my dreams told me this long before I came here. But once I discovered the grimoire, I put it all together. I took a picture of some of the pages and followed my intuition when it came time to make the incantations."

"Ah, brilliant, my dear," Madame Morgan said, raising a glass in the air.

Hannah and Jewelia joined Morgan in a toast, clinking their glasses in celebration.

After dinner, the entire village, including all the festival-goers, gathered around a colossal bonfire. They danced and sang for hours. Jewelia's heart filled with relief, Hannah's heart filled with belonging, and Morgan's heart beamed with pride and gratitude.

After much revelry, each woman grasped a torch, lighting it from the fire, and they began their walk back to the manor. As they walked in a glowing procession, the moon passed over Maple Hollow and the planet Mercury began to accelerate in the sky. Alignments were shifting.

Hannah and Jewelia had moved through a significant challenge in their lives. Hannah would certainly never be the same. Now that she knew what she was capable of, what she was here to do, she would

never go back to the way she was. She was called by
spirit and knew what she was here to do. They must
continue on as Healers of the Hollow. Their existence
spanned multiple dimensions. Their knowledge would
continue to expand with each soul they freed from the
darkness.

But what about the Dream Haunters? They had defeated two, but there were more. And perhaps she had
only freed dreamers who were trapped recently, during this Mercury retrograde period. There were millions of people in the world, each one dreaming every
night—how could just she and her aunt keep everyone
safe from being trapped in their own desolate worlds
of negative energy? Perhaps she was here to activate
knowledge in others who could join in the fight. Was
there a way to transfer her Healer ability to another?
All these questions swirled in Hannah's head as they
walked.

Back at the manor, they approached the family
hearth, each touching her torch to the flame, bringing
the bonfire magick back to their home and resealing
the bonds of heritage and protection. So many different possibilities for her future flashed through Hannah's mind. Were they premonitions, parallel realities,
wishful thinking, or visions of manifestation? Only the
future would tell. For now, they had defeated their
demons and kept the magick of the pumpkin patch
safe.

The moon made its way across the sky. The silence of
the night fell like a thick fog around the island. Nestled
in the firefly glows and the lightning bugs, the crickets
slowly hummed and the crows cawed in the distance.
A breeze gently blew. It was time for them all to go to
sleep, to dreamland.

That night, Hannah had a dream within a dream, in which she woke to the sound of musical notes playing in the distance. She wondered who was playing. *It must be Aunt Jewelia*, she thought.

But as she entered the hallway and passed Jewelia's room, she saw her sleeping in her bed. She descended the stairs and headed toward the great hall where the ornate organ lived, which was now calling her with its ethereal notes. The closer she got, the more curious she became. She wasn't surprised to see that it wasn't someone playing the organ at all. It was Wixby.

"Wixby!" she proclaimed. "I've missed you!" She ran up to the fuzzy cat sitting on the bench, his hind legs extended as his paws reached for the keys.

Whiskers and all, he turned to Hannah, a warm smile across his face. "Hannah, you did it!" he meowed, jumping into her arms. "I knew you could," he went on. "It was inside you all this time." The warmth of his small body filled Hannah's heart with a glow she couldn't remember ever feeling before.

Wixby had been her guide all along. She had finally found her family, her place, her home. "Hollow is Home," she replied, holding him close, caressing his fur. "I'm home."

CHAPTER THIRTY

THE FAMILIARS

NOVEMBER 1, 2007

Hannah greeted Jewelia in the morning light of the kitchen. Midnight had followed her down the stairs, scampering at her heels.

"Good morning, Aunt Jewelia," Hannah chirped.

"Good morning, love," Jewelia sang back.

"Midnight came with me. He follows me everywhere," Hannah said.

"He watches over you. I've had many familiars over time," Jewelia replied. "Before Midnight, it was my beloved Wixby."

"Wixby?" Hannah asked in surprise. Wixby had been real?

"Why, yes. My last feline familiar was named Wixby."

"Wait, what?" Hannah trailed off. She'd thought Wixby existed only in her dreams.

"Let me show you, love," Jewelia said as she reached out her hand for Hannah's and led her into the foyer.

They ascended the stairs together. At the top was the regal painting of Jewelia and Midnight that Hannah had first seen when she arrived at the manor. Jewelia placed her hands gently on the corner of the gilded frame, and began to pull. As she did, the frame began to creak and roll forward. Behind it hung another painting. It was also of Jewelia, in a long velvet dress that grazed the floor. It was also elegant, and regal, but next to her, sitting perched on a small side table, was Wixby!

He looked exactly as he had in Hannah's dreams. "I..." She wasn't sure how to start. "I know Wixby," she finally said.

"You know him?"

"He's come to me in my dreams ever since I've been at the manor. I...I thought he was a figment of my imagination," Hannah explained.

"Oh Wixby, my love! Of course he did," Aunt Jewelia exclaimed, thrilled. "That's wonderful. I'm so glad his spirit reached yours. I hoped my former familiars would come to your aid to help you. He was always such an amazing guide." A smile crossed Jewelia's face. "So now you know another secret about the dreamworld—it's a place where all spirits can gather to guide us. Not just our former felines, either. Any spirit we've known or not known can come to our aid in the land of dreams. It is a magickal place, which most people don't realize. But when we open ourselves up to the guidance the dreamworld offers, we welcome the assistance the universe wants to give us. It's already waiting there for us, we just have to ask. I see Wixby often too, in my dreams. In fact, he came to me when I was trapped. I'm so glad you were able to connect with him. The cats are here to help us on our path as Healers of the Hollow. They, and others such as Mr. Adams, are Protectors of the Hollow. Their duty is to protect the Healers and our legacy. We have many guides, as you will see soon, love."

Jewelia restored the painting to its original state and started walking towards the library. "You may not realize this, love," she continued, "but cats are our spirit companions to the netherworlds. They can walk between worlds very easily. In ancient societies, such as Ancient Egypt, they were considered our guardians, not just of the homestead in general but of our spirits as well. It is part of our legacy and tradition to always have a familiar living with us. They are spirits, like us, in physical form, here to guide us through this realm. We share a special world with them. Have you ever noticed that some people don't like cats or don't understand them?"

"I have," Hannah remarked.

"This is because they are not in touch with their inner world. They are denying their inner sense of knowing, and most likely also denying their dreamworld."

"Ah, I see," Hannah said.

"Cats are experts at seeing in the dark, moving between the veil of the worlds, and existing side by side with mystery. We can draw so much power from them when we allow their magick to be part of our world. There is something between us that cannot be explained in words, although it does make it easier when they actually communicate to us in our own verbal language." She smiled.

"So you know about him talking?" Hannah asked.

"Of course he can talk, love. I knew when he passed on that he had never left me. We only ever need to be willing to listen."

CHAPTER THIRTY-ONE

THE LEGACY

"I have more to show you, my dear." Jewelia beckoned Hannah to follow her into the library. As they entered, she went straight to a bookshelf and grabbed a large volume off the wall. She opened the ancient book and pointed to a map. "As you have learned, this island is a vortex. It is an energy center that draws other energies from everywhere. This year was very unique because of the rare synchronicity of Halloween and Mercury retrograde. The thinning veil combined with the planetary influence created a portal that allowed the Dream Haunters to traverse the boundary that usually exists between the worlds and shapeshift into ours. They were able to use this to their advantage.

"As Healers of the Hollow, we must prepare for the next time. We must be ready for them, as our work is never done. Each retrograde they will trap more people, the more powerful they become. This is why we must educate the world, so they become aware of the danger and of their own power to reverse it. The majority of the world is literally walking around with blinders on. They don't listen to the messages of their dreams and can't see their own power if you put it in their hands. We live in a world that has separated us from our inner wisdom, so much so that we unknowingly have strengthened the powers of the Dream Haunters, giving them free reign to trap us as they choose. Together, this is our duty now," Aunt Jewelia continued. "We must combine our forces to raise everyone else's awareness. We must step outside of our family legacy and secret past, stop hiding our truths, and step into the larger world so we can really start helping others. We can no longer stay hidden. The time has come to reveal ourselves and help others traverse their dreamworld for the better."

Hannah nodded, understanding both the call she must now answer and the legacy she must now embody. As Jewelia placed the book back on the shelf, Hannah's eyes drifted to another volume nearby. She found herself reaching for the book and reading the title on the spine: *Vibration Frequencies: Aligning for Activation.* As she held it in her hands, it naturally flipped open to the right section, which read, *The frequency of 396 Hz is a fear liberator, bringing feelings of safety and security. 432 Hz is a healing miracle frequency which aligns us with the universe. And the resonance of 963 Hz has the power to open our minds, improve our sleep, and raise our consciousness.*

She then flipped to the next page which displayed a diagram of piano keys. She matched up each resonance to the corresponding piano keys. "396 is G4, 432 is A4, and 963 is B5!" she said out loud, shocking even herself with her intuitive prowess. "Of course!" she exclaimed, a shimmering feeling of validation and vibration surrounding her.

"Is that how you saved me?" Jewelia asked, her eyes widening as Hannah's smile began to sparkle.

"Yes!" Hannah proclaimed with pride. She had tapped her inner knowing, harnessed the power of sound, and healed her aunt. "But there's just one thing left I don't understand," she added. "Why was Morgan trapped by the Dream Haunters? And since she knew how the pumpkin portal worked, why was I the only one who could save you?" she asked.

Aunt Jewelia smiled and shook her head. "Remember love, you *are* the key. There comes a time in everyone's journey when they must embrace their power. It is an unspoken rule of the universe. Morgan was able to guide you toward your realization, but her powers are different than ours. It is together that we are most powerful."

"I see...I could live here with you and you can teach me everything I need to know. We can continue together, to make sure neither of us ever get trapped again."

Aunt Jewelia reached into her pocket and pulled out a silver chain, from which dangled a small skeleton key. "I want you to have this, my love, to always remind you that you are the key." Her eyes glowed from the depths of her soul. She motioned to Hannah to allow her to clasp the necklace around her neck. A peaceful smile passed over her lips and she enveloped Hannah in a deep, comforting hug. "Yes, Hannah, this is your home."

EPILOGUE
PUMPKIN ILLUMINATION

As the sun began to set in the distance, Hannah, Jewelia, and Morgan gathered in the pumpkin patch. They were followed by the quick small paws of Merlin, Milu, and Midnight. Mystera and Wixby followed close behind in spirit. As they proceeded down the cypress-lined path to the patch, bats weaved against the black silhouettes of the trees, starting their dance into darkness.

Once in the patch, Jewelia instructed everyone to select a pumpkin still on the vine. "Pick one that resonates with you," she advised. "It will call to you, and you just have to be willing to hear it."

One by one they selected their pumpkins, lifting them up from the ground with the vines intact. A visible electricity passed from the pumpkins and the vines into their hands.

"*Expergiscimini Vineas*," Hannah proclaimed as the vines began to wrap around their legs and arms. A low, thick fog began to shroud the patch.

Each woman chanted to herself with her eyes closed. Merlin and Milu stood like statues at Morgan's feet, watching. Midnight wrapped his tail around Jewelia's right ankle. Mystera glowed with a warmth that blended with Hannah's aura. Wixby sat atop the largest pumpkin in the patch with a smile as wide as his tiny furry face. As the moon began to rise brightly on the horizon, the wind blew in the trees. Orange, red, and golden maple leaves scattered and swirled all around them in a slow and magickal autumnal funnel. The vines began to pulsate, their deep green hues turning to a sparkling gold. The pumpkins began to glow, as if illuminated from the inside with eternal flames.

Then all at once, the three women, the three cats, and Mystera and Wixby disappeared. The patch was silent once again.

ACKNOWLEDGMENTS

I would like to send love and light to my late father, who recognized my potential and encouraged me to pursue English Literature, and whose passing confirmed the existence of realms beyond the veil; to my mother, who fostered my childhood love of Halloween with her creatively handmade costumes; to my sister, for always making me laugh even in the darkest of times; and to my Irish and Scottish ancestors, for guiding me from the other side. My beta reader friends, who contributed to refining the story to its fullest, also deserve my heartfelt thanks. Lastly, to dreams: may you hear their whispers and follow their wisdom.

ABOUT THE AUTHOR

Metaphysical author Megan Mary, a dream analyst, intuitive, and mystic, intertwines her passion for personal transformation, magick, and cats with the ethereal realm of dreams.

In addition to a career spanning over twenty-five years creating, managing and marketing websites, she holds a BA and an MA in English Literature, certification in British Studies, is pursuing her PhD in Metaphysical Sciences and is a member of the International Association for the Study of Dreams.

After being diagnosed with three chronic illnesses, she experienced a spiritual awakening. She now empowers women all over the world to live more authentic, aligned, and abundant lives through dream empowerment and mystical guidance. Her podcast, Women's Dream Enlightenment, has been voted as one of the Top 20 Spiritual Awakening Podcasts You Must Follow. When she's not dreaming or weaving digital webs, she enjoys spending time with her husband and two magickal cats.

Visit MeganMary.com & Follow Megan Mary on X, Youtube, Instagram, Pintrest, Tiktok & GoodReads.

Dear Reader,

I hope you've enjoyed the first book of the series. If you'd like to be part of the Witches of Maple Hollow Community, I invite you to sign up for my newsletter at MeganMary.com, where you'll receive special email notifications as new books in this series are released, beta reader opportunities, and more. I also hope you'll consider dropping a quick review at the retailer of your choice as well as on GoodReads. Coming Spring 2025: The Dream Mirrors, Book 2 of the Witches of Maple Hollow series!

I love to chat with other women who are intrigued by metaphysics and who wish to delve into the meaning of their dreams. Please reach out and share your experience—I'd love to hear it. Download a free dream journal template at MeganMary.com. Thank you again for your support.

Megan Mary

Made in the USA
Columbia, SC
02 October 2024

7a45d020-e457-400f-9a8d-6077e4cdd1ccR01